G000161629

Published novels:

Historical

Kitty McKenzie
Kitty McKenzie's Land
Southern Sons
To Gain What's Lost
Isabelle's Choice
Nicola's Virtue
Aurora's Pride
Grace's Courage
Eden's Conflict
Catrina's Return
Where Rainbow's End
Broken Hero
The Promise of Tomorrow
The Slum Angel

Marsh Saga Series

Millie

Contemporary

Long Distance Love
Hooked on You
Where Dragonflies Hover (Dual Timeline)

Short Stories

A New Dawn
Art of Desire
What He Taught Her

Christmas at the Chateau

AnneMarie Brear

Chapter One

Chateau Dumont, Northern France
December 1920

Millie, Lady Remington, wrapped her baby
son, Jonathan, in a blanket and picked him up.
He was fed and washed and smelled fresh and
clean. 'So, young man. You've been such a good
boy and grown so much and so fast, you've been
allowed downstairs to socialise with your
family. They've all come from England to see
you and spend Christmas with us.' She kissed
his soft plump cheek. He had soft downy hair
and she wondered if he'd have her dark curls
when older.

Walking past the cumbersome incubator, the
hired unit that had saved Jonathan's life and
kept him alive these last seven weeks, she gave it
a friendly pat as she always did.

It was unusual to have a hospital baby
incubator in a private home, but her father-in-
law, Jacques, had known someone at a hospital
in Paris and favours were exchanged.

The kind gesture to hire the unique unit made life so much more bearable as they could stay home at the chateau and not travel to the hospital in Paris.

Jonathan's premature birth had followed another birth, which had ended in sorrow as her first baby was too small to survive. But not this time. Despite being born early and living in an incubator, Jonathan had thrived. To her and Jeremy he was their miracle baby.

With a nod and a smile to Nursé Allard, a middle-aged au pair they employed to help with the care of Jonathan, Millie left the nursery and carried her darling son across the gallery and passed the bedrooms of the chateau's left wing. She felt confident that the bedrooms were as comfortable as she and her limited staff could make them. They had worked for weeks making sure the bedrooms had new beds, linens, and warm fires lit.

After being occupied by Germans during the war and subsequently bombed they were lucky half of the chateau was habitable. If the plaster-work was coming away from the walls, or the wallpaper was peeling, and the windows were stubbornly stuck, what did it matter?

Her family knew the chateau had been through a war, and Millie and Jeremy were doing their best to restore it to its former glory as it had been in Jeremy's mother's time.

The buzz of noise met her at the double doorway of the Grand Salon; the first room to have its renovations completed.

As members of her family saw her, they cried in happiness and hurried to peek at the new arrival they'd not yet seen.

'Oh, he's so tiny, Millie!' Mama crooned as she took him in her arms. 'And you look so well, too, daughter.'

'He's gorgeous!' Prue, her beautiful and wayward sister, touched his little cheek.

'Can I have a hold, Mama?' Cece, her youngest sister asked, her blue eyes soft with devotion for the baby.

'In a moment. I've only just got him.' Mama sat beside Grandmama. 'Look, Mother, isn't he adorable?'

'Of course, he is. We don't have ugly babies in this family.' Grandmama peered at him over her glasses. 'He's a fighter is that one. He'll go far. You see if he doesn't.'

Mama kissed Jonathan's head, her eyes misty. 'I wish your grandpapa was here to see you. How he would have loved having a grandson.'

Prue nodded. 'And the way Cece and I are going, he'll be the only one!'

'Speak for yourself!' Cece snapped. 'I will have children. You, on the other hand, who knows?'

Millie went to stand beside Jeremy near the roaring fire and his arm snaked around her waist. 'He's going to be spoilt.'

Jeremy shrugged, his handsome face breaking into a smile. 'Let them. They've waited seven weeks to see him because of the colds they all suffered. They've kept away until they were better, and he was stronger. A few hours of cuddles isn't going to harm him. Besides, he'll not see them every day as he grows up, so what harm does it do if he gets spoilt when they are here.'

'*And* it's Christmas.' She gazed up at him, feeling full of love and contentment.

'*And* it's Christmas.' He gave her a kiss that tingled her skin and warmed her heart.

Since Jonathan's dramatic early birth, Jeremy had suffered episodes of recurring shell shock inflicted from fighting in the war. The stress of willing Jonathan to survive had played heavily on Jeremy's mind, causing him to have his nightmares again. However, they were coping with them and taking each day as it came.

The bell rang at the front door, and Millie waited to see who had arrived. Sophie, one of the girls who helped in the chateau, brought in Monsieur Jacques Baudin, the estate's champagne exporter. A charming older Frenchman, who recently learned he was Jeremy's biological father.

In the seven weeks since Millie had told both men the truth of their relationship, which she'd learned from letters she'd read belonging to Jeremy's mother, Camile, their friendship had been strained.

The natural bond they'd always enjoyed had been dealt a blow and both Jeremy and Jacques needed time to adjust to the news. Jacques threw himself into his work of exporting the chateau's champagne, and Jeremy devoted his time to rebuilding the chateau and the vineyard, determined to recreate the high standard of champagne Chateau Dumont was known for before the war.

'Welcome, Jacques.' Millie kissed his cheeks in turn.

'*Joyeux Noel, mon cher!*'

'Joyeux Noel. Your dear wife is not with you?'

'Non, she remains with her own sister who is frail and very ill. I was sent here to be kept out of the way. My wife sends her apologies.'

Millie wondered if Jacques' wife ever really wanted to be in their company but remained tight-lipped about it. Still, something didn't seem right about that particular marriage. 'You remember my sister, Prue, from when she was here last summer?'

'I do indeed. How could I forget such a lovely *mademoiselle*?' He bowed over Prue's hand and she jumped up to kiss both his cheeks.

'Lovely to see you again, Jacques.'

'And this is my grandmama, Mrs Adeline Fordham, my mama, Mrs Violet Marsh, and my other sister Cecelia, though we call her Cece.'

'What a delightful array of beautiful women!' Jacques bowed over each hand. '*Enchanté!*'

'You do look like Jeremy, doesn't he, Mama?' Prue said. 'I don't know how I didn't spot it when I was here for the summer.'

A moment of stillness came over the room. Mama took a deep breath and gave Prue a fierce look.

'What?' Prue stared at everyone. 'The secret is out so why pretend they aren't related?'

'Absolutely.' Jacques rubbed his short clipped grey beard. 'I am honoured to have such a fine-looking son, and if he resembles me then what can I say?'

He grinned mischievously. 'And my grandson will be even more handsome than either of us.' He bent to softly touch the top of the baby's head.

'Excellently said,' Grandmama nodded. 'And although both Jacques and Jeremy are adequately handsome, I do believe the striking dark good looks come from my side of the family.'

'What does that say about me, being the only ginger-haired one in the family?' Cece asked.

Grandmama gave her a look of sympathy. 'Well my dear, you take after your father, and poor Lionel was of the fairer tribe. You can't be blamed for that. He obviously had some Scottish lineage,' she said it as though it was a fate worse than death.

'And what's wrong with being blonde?' Prue pouted with a laugh. 'It's done me no harm.' She touched her stylish short cut.

'Oh yes,' Cece muttered, 'we all know you got the lovely hair and is the prettiest amongst us.'

'Drinks!' Jeremy quietly refilled everyone's glasses as the baby was passed from one lap to the other.

Millie sat next to Grandmama, who sipped madeira and watched Cece cooing over Jonathan.

'She is good with babies,' Grandmama said, indicating Cece. 'I've seen her with friends' babies and small children, and she has a natural gift with them.'

'She does, but perhaps not Prue.' Millie laughed and glanced at her sister who was chatting away to Jacques, and not making a fuss over the baby as Cece was.

'No, well at least not yet.' Grandmama gave a shrug. 'She's got a lot of living to do first. Prue is much like me. I wasn't very maternal. I wasn't sure I even wanted children.'

'Really?'

'Your mother and Uncle Hugo were enough for me. I told your grandfather that there would be no more babies and made sure it didn't happen.' She gave Millie a sidelong look. 'You do know how to prevent them from happening, don't you?'

Millie blushed and lowered her voice. 'Yes, Grandmama, I do. Jeremy and I have discussed it.'

'And you have the "*French letter*" as they are called. Marvellous invention they are.'

'Grandmama!' Millie whispered harshly. 'Yes, it's all taken care of.'

'Good! And don't be so prudish, my girl, you sound like your mother. You're a married woman, I'm only talking of natural things between a husband and wife. If Queen Victoria could talk of sex last century, then so golly well will I now!'

Millie shook her head, her grandmama was a law unto herself. 'Thank you for your concern, but it's all been taken care of.'

'Then I'll leave well enough alone.'

'Thank you.'

'But I would hate to see you tied down with half a dozen little monsters around your skirts.'

'I don't see Jonathan as a little monster.'

'You will do. Children can be so selfish, always wanting attention. It drains you. Although,' Grandmama took a sip of her drink, 'I'm informed that at least you have a decent nanny, which helps a lot.'

'Yes, we like her very much.'

'And your mother tells me she is middle-aged. Excellent.'

'Oh yes she has much experience and has worked in England, so she has very good English.'

'I'm not talking about her skills, I'm talking about the woman herself. You were smart to get an older woman.'

'Why?'

'Good Lord, girl. Think on it a moment.' She lowered her voice. 'A young, pretty slender nanny living under the same roof as your husband, or any male guest you may have. Well, the temptation can be too much.'

'Jeremy would never betray me with a member of staff, or anyone.'

'No, he may not, but at least don't tempt fate by hiring a young slip of a thing with doe-eyes and a soft voice.' Grandmama took another sip of madeira. 'I've seen it many times before. Before you know it, the slim young nanny suddenly has a large stomach and is out the door. Very upsetting for all concerned.'

'Grandmama, really!'

'I'm just saying, that's all.' Grandmama waved her glass in the air. 'Men love a woman in uniform – sends them crazy. In my younger years I had a dress-up box filled to the brim. Enormous fun.'

'Grandmama!' Millie nearly choked on her drink.

'Mother! Are you being outrageous again?' Mama demanded to know.

'Prudes.' Grandmama snorted and finished her drink. 'Jeremy, fill me up again, there's a good man. I must say the chateau looks better than I was expecting. Your mama thought it would be close to a ruin.'

'It seemed liked it when we first arrived. Every room was in such a state. The Germans had painted propaganda over the walls, smashed and burnt furniture, stripped the carpets.'

'Beasts.'

'Then as you must have seen when you arrived, the right wing is still very damaged. We've boarded it up for now, and in time we'll repair it, but for now it'll stay as it is until we get the estate producing profitably again.'

'That won't take long, my dear. Everyone loves to drink champagne.'

The doorbell rang again and as it was being answered, Nursé Allard came and stood in the doorway, waiting to take the baby back upstairs.

After Grandmama's talk, Millie reappraised the nurse as an ideal nanny, efficient, good-natured, kind and not slender, or young or doe-eyed. Millie congratulated herself on making the right choice, even if it was unbeknown.

Kisses goodnight were given to Jonathan and Millie held him as Monty Pattison entered the room.

Her stomach did a little twist at the sight of him. It had been nearly eight months since she'd seen their English estate manager at Remington Court in Yorkshire.

Her friendship with him was hard to define. At first, she had hated him, blaming him for being dependent on Jeremy and becoming Jeremy's friend so soon after they were married.

When Jeremy suffered the worst of his shell shock it was Monty he turned to not Millie, making her feel alone and unwanted. Then when Jeremy went for treatment in Plymouth, she and Monty were thrown together.

Monty had been there for her when she lost the first baby, and she had listened to him tell his story of being badly wounded in the jaw and neck during the war and losing everything he loved after that. By the time she'd left Remington Court in his safe hands to rekindle her relationship with Jeremy, she and Monty had become somewhat friends, despite him telling her he was half in love with her.

'Monty, dear chap!' Jeremy shook his hand vigorously. 'So happy you travelled all this way to spend Christmas with us.'

'Thank you for inviting me, Sir Jeremy. I never thought I would visit northern France again, to be honest with you. But I am pleased to spend Christmas with you all and not alone at Remington Court.'

'How is everything going in Yorkshire?'

'The estate is doing well.'

Millie paused in front of Monty with Jonathan. 'No talk of business tonight. Meet our son instead.'

Monty gazed first at Millie then at Jonathan. 'He is a beautiful baby, Lady Remington. I'm so happy to see he is growing well.'

She smiled lovingly down at her baby. 'He's strong. A survivor.'

'Like his mother, I suspect.'

Millie blushed and walked away, giving the baby to his nurse, who scooted out of the room and back upstairs.

With Monty welcomed and a drink shoved in his hand, the room became more like a party, especially when Prue wound up the gramophone and played some new jazz records she'd brought with her, especially ordered from America.

Millie watched Prue dance with Jacques, who once more fell under Prue's engaging spell, as most men did, young or old.

Prue wore a drop waist dress of light green, with strands of beads around her neck, her short blonde hair had a long feather pinned to the side and she had make-up on which Mama disapproved of. She looked chic and stylish and full of life. She couldn't help it and the family adored her all the more because she was so unconcerned by her own vivacity.

Whereas Cece was the opposite to Prue and Millie felt a little sorry for her youngest sister.

With red hair and pale skin, Cece, although pretty, had none of Prue's high-spiritedness. Like all the Marsh sisters they had the blue eyes of their mother, but Cece was quiet, even quieter than Millie.

What's more, Cece didn't care for fashion and dancing and all the other things young women of her age should be interested in.

Millie worried for her, and now as she watched Cece smile and listen devotedly to every word Monty uttered, Millie was only too aware that her sister was still very much in love with Monty since first meeting him last Christmas.

Prue allowed Jacques to take a rest and she put music on that was slower.

Millie walked over to her, away from everyone else. 'You seem happy. I take it you've had no word from Win?'

'None at all. I told you months ago it was all finished.'

'I'm glad.' Millie was relieved that the brief flirtation Prue had shared with a married man called Win, someone Millie had never met, was over and done with. 'I was worried that when you left here at the end of summer you'd meet back up with him.'

'I promised you I wouldn't, and I haven't.'

Millie studied her sister. Since her family arrived this afternoon, Prue seemed edgier than normal almost as though she was waiting for something to happen or searching for something to happen. 'You would tell me if anything was troubling you, wouldn't you?'

Prue frowned and changed the record. 'Of course, but there isn't. I'm perfectly happy.'

'Truly?' Millie persisted.

A large smile spread across Prue's face. 'Absolutely. Now stop fussing. It's Christmas and time to have some fun.'

Vivian, their housekeeper and at the moment also the cook, came into the room and announced dinner was served.

As the family moved into the dining room, or *salle á dîner*, as the room was officially called, Millie gave an eye to the decorations. The room looked beautiful and she was proud to admit it.

Millie, Vivian and Catrin and Sophie, the two girls that helped in the chateau, had spent days creating a Christmas theme throughout the house.

Holly sprigs were hung over every mantelpiece and the fireplaces all burned scented wood from fallen orchard trees that Jeremy had ordered to be cut up, ready for the new planting of fruit trees when the soil thawed after winter. Candelabras sat on every table surface and held tall candles adding a festive light to the new chandeliers, which now hung from the few rooms their team of builders had completed.

With everyone seated, Jeremy at the head of the table and Millie at his opposite end, she felt an incredible sense of happiness and love.

Vivian and the girls brought through platter after platter of delicious food; meats, salads, potatoes, vegetables and bread.

Wine was drunk, and the conversation was light.

Happy smiling faces greeted her everywhere she looked. This would be a wonderful Christmas.

Chapter Two

Cece dressed with care, choosing a warm navy skirt and matching cardigan over a white blouse. Thick stockings and solid black shoes completed the outfit. Satisfied she looked well and would be warm enough to go outside to select a Christmas tree for decorating, she left the bedroom she shared with Prue.

Her heart somersaulted as she passed the bedroom she knew Monty was sharing with Jacques. She paused, listening for any sound behind the door but all was quiet.

Continuing on, she replayed in her mind the evening before when Monty arrived. She'd known of his coming as Millie had told her a month ago in a letter and Cece had immediately written to Monty to urge him to accept the invitation to Chateau Dumont for Christmas.

At the top of the staircase she stopped, again listening, listening for Monty's deep voice and the thrill it always gave her when she heard it.

For a year, since last Christmas when they had met at Remington Court, she had wanted no man but Monty. Even with his battle scars, which disfigured his jaw and neck, his quiet reserved nature and his lack of encouragement, she had thought of no one but him.

When he agreed to write to her she'd nearly burst with excitement. His letters arrived weekly without fail. No one could ever say they were love letters, for they were not. There was no sentiment in them at all. But they were his words to her, his thoughts to her and she treasured each one as though they spoke of a hidden love, which of course they didn't.

However, she wouldn't give up all hope. He must think something of her or why else would he write to her each week? It was frustrating that Millie and Jeremy had moved to France at the start of last summer because she had no reason now to go to Remington Court, where Monty lived, managing the estate on their behalf. The letters had to be enough, except for the one time he agreed to meet her in York for afternoon tea.

The few hours they spent together were the best of her life. She knew she had talked too much, trying to make up for his lack of conversation. It had been shortly after Millie lost her first baby and gone to London to reunite with Jeremy. Monty had seemed withdrawn, but courteous and friendly in the quiet way she had come to expect from him.

'There you are!' Prue snapped from the bottom of the staircase, already wearing her coat and boots. 'We've been waiting for you. What on earth has taken you so long, for heaven's sake?'

'Sorry.' Cece hurried down the stairs and went along the corridor that led to the boot room and the doors at the back of the chateau. She quickly donned her hat, scarf and coat and tugged on her brown walking boots.

Outside, a cold wind blew, and the grey pewter sky threatened snow.

'It's freezing!' Cece laughed at Monty, who waited by a former ambulance used in the Great War. Jeremy had bought the ambulance and had stripped it bare to just the tray at the back for use on the vineyard. Today it was taking them over to a nearby farm, which had pine trees for sale to cut as Christmas trees.

'Is Millie not coming with us?' she asked Prue as they climbed into the truck. It was a squash, but they managed to fit in — just.

Jeremy started the engine. 'No, she's staying home with your mother and grandmother. Jonathan is awake and needs feeding.'

'Millie should put him on the bottle.' Prue hitched up closer to Monty, which annoyed Cece. 'She's tied to that nursery.'

Jeremy set off round the courtyard and down a back drive towards a side entrance of the estate. 'It's better for Jonathan to have her milk than a powdered milk. He needs all the help he can get starting off so small.'

'Well done to Millie,' Cece agreed. She'd love to have a baby, in fact several of them. She adored children and couldn't wait to be married and a mother. She glanced at Monty, but he was looking out of the window at the passing rows of leafless grape vines.

'Oh, it's snowing!' Prue suddenly announced. 'How wonderful! Jacques said it would do so today.'

Cece glowered at her. In her opinion Prue was a little too enthusiastic when it came to Jeremy's father. Monsieur Baudin was a handsome man, that couldn't be denied, but he was married and an old man. Prue was making a fool of herself, always laughing at his flattery and preening like a peacock whenever his gaze fell on her. Cece was glad she wasn't like that. She felt a blush creep up her neck at the thought of acting in such a way in front of Monty.

Did men like that simpering and false coy behavior? Surely not. She was sure Monty didn't. Perhaps it was only Frenchmen that enjoyed all that flirting and silliness.

They rumbled down a rutted farm track to an ancient farmhouse of pale stone and stopped the truck. The wind died down and the snow fell gently in large flakes. Jeremy spoke to the farmer, who gestured for them to take his handsaw that he had left on a wheelbarrow beside an outbuilding.

As the little troupe followed him down a track and into a sparse woodland, Cece stared at the damage done by the war.

Huge craters pitted the fields. Many of the trees had been blown up, leaving just broken trunks pointing up like toothpicks. She thought of all the men who had died in this area and shivered. Despite the war being over for a couple of years, the army were still finding bodies of buried soldiers and she hoped they wouldn't stumble across one today.

'Are you cold?' Monty asked her.

Cece smiled, happy that he was concerned. 'Only a little.'

'We'll get you chopping then, that'll warm you up,' he replied.

She'd rather he warmed her up but remained silent.

Through the ruined woodland they walked until they reached a small plantation of immature pine trees, which miraculously had survived the bombings and battles. Here the farmer spoke in rapid French to Jeremy, who nodded and answered and then shook the man's hand.

'Well,' Jeremy said, studying the squat trees around them. 'We can take our pick.'

'That one looks good.' Prue instantly pointed to large tree to their right. It was the tallest in the plantation.

Monty chuckled. 'That'll not fit in the Grand Salon.'

'Will it not? But the salon's ceiling is so high.'

'And so is that tree!' he joked with her.

Prue shook her head, dislodging snow off her hat. 'I really think we need a good size tree.'

'You'll need a ladder to decorate the top branches.'

'So?' Prue shrugged, then grinned. 'Or you could hoist me onto your shoulder?' she said saucily.

Cece stamped her feet to keep them warm, hating the easiness with which Prue could flirt with almost anyone, young or old. 'How about this one?' Cece pointed to the tree closest to her without really looking at it.

Jeremy walked around it, wiping some of the snow off the branches. 'No, it's not even on this side. Millie wouldn't want that one.'

Monty moved away and disappeared behind another tree. 'This seems a perfect one.'

They joined him and agreed. The tree was wide at the bottom and grew straight, but not too tall.

'It's about seven foot.' Jeremy nodded. 'Perfect.'

While Jeremy and Monty set about chopping the tree down, Cece and Prue stood together, trying to keep warm. The snow was falling heavier now, whitening the landscape.

The chopping of the axe was the only sound. A final crack and the tree toppled over.

Jeremy wiped his brow beneath his hat. 'We need the truck down here, otherwise we'll have to drag this the whole way back to the farm.'

Prue laughed. 'Why didn't we think of that first?'

'Because we weren't sure these trees would be suitable or that the truck could make it down here, but I think it will. The ground is quite hard.'

'I'll go bring the truck down,' Monty said turning away.

'Wait, can I do it?' Cece surprised herself more than anyone when she spoke.

'You?' Prue frowned. 'You can't drive.'

'I can. Sort of. I've been practicing.'

'How? Mama doesn't own a motor car.'

Cece squirmed under their attention. 'No, she doesn't but our neighbours, the Livingstones, do. I've been learning to drive with their new chauffer, Jimmy.'

'Really?' Astonishment raised Prue's voice. 'Will he show me, too?'

'I suppose.' Cece sighed. She didn't want Prue learning to drive. She wanted that to be her thing. True, Millie could drive but she lived in France. Cece wanted to be the only one in the family in England to have a skill no one else had.

'I'll come with you,' Monty said. 'Just in case you need help.'

Instantly Cece felt better. 'Thank you.'

Having Monty to herself, even for just a short time, was exciting.

As they trudged back up to the farm, she wanted to say something witty and funny, but her mind went blank.

'I do love the snow,' Monty said, looking up into the sky. Snowflakes fell on his face and he grinned.

'I like it better when I'm inside,' Cece mumbled, slipping a little.

Monty took her elbow. 'I'm impressed you're willing to drive this old truck.'

'I like to test myself sometimes.'

'Interesting.'

She didn't know what he meant by that. Was she interesting? Or was her being able to drive interesting?

They reached the truck and Monty wiped the fallen snow off the windscreen, then wound the crank-shaft.

Nervously, Cece got behind the wheel and started the engine. She gave a thumbs up to Monty, who jumped in beside her.

'There's no clear defined track, you realise?' Monty grinned.

'I'll follow our footprints.' She put it into gear, grinding them a little and they jumped forward.

Monty, sitting on the edge of his seat, peered out the snowy window. 'Come over to your left... That's right.'

'Right?' Cece jerked the wheel. 'I need to go right?'

'No, left! Left!' Monty laughed.

They bumped along the field, the snow hiding the holes and ruts. Cece pressed her foot down more to speed the truck up.

'Not too fast!' Monty glanced at her in alarm.

'We can't hurt anything.' She bit her lip to stop from smiling too much. 'If I can drive in the busy streets of York I can certainly drive in a field!'

The wheels went into several holes and a small ditch, making them bounce on the seat and the truck groan.

'Change down a gear,' Monty instructed, his hat white with snowflakes.

The windscreen wipers didn't work very well, and snow was gathering quickly. Winding down her window, Cece had to lean out to see clearly. Snow pelted her face, stinging her skin.

'Turn through those two broken trunks,' Monty called.

She did her best, nearly hitting the one on her side, but she made it through and into the woodland. Here, the snow was caught higher up in the branches and fell less hard.

Slowly she edged the truck through the trees to the small pine plantation and pulled the vehicle to a stop.

'That was great driving in these conditions,' Monty declared, opening the door.

Her shoulders ached a bit from the tension of concentrating but she felt such a sense of pride that she jumped down, grinning like a child. 'I did it!'

'Well done!' Prue ran up and hugged her. 'I'm so proud of you! Wait until we tell Millie that you drove a truck in the snow across fields.'

'Excellent work, Cece.' Jeremy gave her a wink as he pulled the fallen tree closer to the back of the truck. 'Your mama won't be happy with me allowing you to do that.'

'I'm a grown woman. If Millie can drive, then so can I.'

All four of them hoisted the tree onto the back of the truck and climbed in again, squashed and laughing.

'I can't feel my toes,' Prue moaned, her cheeks red.

'A hot toddy is what we need,' Jeremy said, driving the truck away from the farm and into the chateau's estate.

'A hot bath more like.' Cece, crushed between Monty and Prue, felt joyful. She glanced at Monty and he smiled back at her. She felt her heart would burst.

Chapter Three

Millie relaxed back against the sofa and listened to the conversations going on around her. After another superb dinner, they had all retired to the Grand Salon with wine, coffee and cheese. They'd spent the afternoon decorating the Christmas tree and it stood in the entrance hall looking magnificent.

Jeremy sat beside her and took her hand. 'Is Jonathan settled?'

'Yes, Nursé Allard was changing him as I left the nursery. He fed well again this evening. He's becoming very greedy.'

'That's my good little man,' Jeremy said smugly.

'He's likely to be asleep now. Mama has cuddled him in front of the fire all afternoon. He's terribly spoilt.'

'He's her grandson, let her spoil him. Soon they will all be gone back to England, and he'll just have us.'

Grandmama walked past and settled herself in a wing-backed chair near the fire, Jacques in the one opposite her. 'No, I do not understand it at all,' she said to him. 'Who is this little man, Gandhi? What makes him so special to cause such unrest in India?'

'Reform, my dear *madame*.' Jacques topped up her wine.

Millie leaned closer to Jeremy to whisper, 'Poor Jacques will have a hard time arguing this subject with Grandmama.'

'I have nothing with which to distract them either,' he whispered back.

Grandmama sat stiffly upright, a known sign to her family she was ready for a good argument. 'Reform? What utter nonsense. Most Indians are suitably grateful to the British Crown. If they weren't why would they have joined us to fight in the war? That would have been the perfect time to flex their independent muscle.'

'The war is over, *madame*,' Jacques said patiently. 'India now looks to their own leaders to fight for their own rights in their own country.'

'But to cause such riots? It's disgraceful. My son, Hugo, is in India working for the British Government and he writes to me about the unrest, and Gandhi is at the head of it all.'

'Gandhi is a non-violent man. He preaches peace. He does not want the riots to happen. Unfortunately, not all of his followers feel the same.'

'Yet, he takes advantage of the unrest to further his own ideals. No good will come of any of this, you mark my words.'

'Let us hope for a successful outcome, *oui*?'

'The British Government needs to take a stand on this issue and the Indians should be grateful.'

'Grateful for what? Being poor, downtrodden, struggling under the British yoke?'

'Not all are poor and downtrodden let me assure you of that. In the past I have met many Indian nobility and they have riches beyond your wildest imagination.'

'It is a small minority, *madame*.'

'Well, you are a Frenchman, you are bound to be biased against us.'

Jacques shrugged his shoulders and raised his hands. 'Politics is a messy business.'

Grandmama snorted in dismissal. 'If it's not the Indians, it's the Irish causing trouble again. It's as though Britain has to continually keep fighting. It's not to be borne. Where would any of those countries be without the might of British commerce helping their people?'

Jacques looked helplessly to Millie and Jeremy.

Millie jumped up. 'Grandmama, it's Christmas let us not talk of politics. Jacques is a Frenchman, and British Rule isn't terribly important to him.'

'It would be if it started to affect your champagne exports.' Grandmama nodded wisely and sipped her wine. 'After all, I suspect there are a great many British and *Indians* who import your cases of Chateau Dumont Champagne in India, are there not, monsieur?'

'Indeed, *madame*.'

'And what of this silly notion in America of prohibition?'

Jacques groaned. 'A disaster. One of our largest markets gone!'

Grandmama leaned forward. 'And what of the black market? You can't tell me that not one American has touched a drop of alcohol since the law came in?'

Jacques also leaned in closer, a wicked glint in his eyes. 'Black market? *Non!* I would do nothing to shame the house of Dumont, *madame*.'

Grandmama chuckled and slapped his knee. 'How glorious!' She turned to Millie and Jeremy. 'Oh, I do love a bit of intrigue. I must know it all.'

Jeremy stiffened slightly. 'There is nothing to tell.'

'You lie!' Grandmama snorted. 'Millie, what do you know?'

Millie squirmed. She knew that Jeremy and Jacques had a secret operation of getting shipments of their champagne across the Atlantic.

'You're blushing, girl, which means you know a lot.'

Jacques topped up Grandmama's glass. 'Let us just say, *madame*, that there may be hidden cellars containing champagne from Chateau Dumont in certain houses in America.'

'Excellent! Beat the authorities at their own game. Bunch of old kites, the lot of them. Why shouldn't people enjoy themselves with a nice drink or two?' Grandmama leaned back in the chair.

'It mustn't become common knowledge, Grandmama,' Millie warned.

'I know when to keep my mouth closed, my dear. I am a master at it.'

Jeremy added wood to the fire. 'Prohibition is only one of the problems we face. The French government are upping the taxes, the borders are closed with Austria, Poland and Hungary and obviously Germany, our biggest export market before the war, is reeling with high exchange rates and taxes. Other countries like Canada are exploring the idea of full prohibition as well. We have to fight for every crate we sell.'

'Then look closer to home, dear boy,' Grandmama said. 'The French guzzle the stuff like it's water. Stop looking for overseas sellers and fill the restaurants and cities here in France. Wealthy people are always wanting to find ways to impress people so make Chateau Dumont Champagne the next "must have".'

Jacques and Jeremy looked at one another and Millie smiled.

Satisfied she'd got her opinion across, Grandmama settled back and sipped more of her drink. 'Have Prue put some music on. You really do need a piano here, Millie, for Cece to play.'

'It's on the list of things to purchase, Grandmama.' Millie went to the gramophone and selected a record.

'I'll have one sent over for you. It'll look very well in that corner over there by the window and near the door. Jonathan should learn to play it, too.'

Millie raised her eyebrows. 'He's seven weeks old.'

'And he should grow up in a house where there is music, and not just the stuff that comes out of that machine!' Grandmama scoffed.

Millie took a deep breath and placed a record on and lowered the needle. As music filled the room she wandered over to where Mama, Monty, Cece and Prue were playing cards. 'What shall you all do tomorrow before the Christmas ball?'

'Let us take the train to Paris and do some shopping,' Prue suggested, playing a card.

'Not in this weather.' Cece placed her card down. 'It was still snowing while we were having dinner, I could see the flakes hitting the window.'

Prue studied the cards in her hand. 'It might be all gone by morning. Isn't Jacques' wife arriving for Christmas?'

'No, she is staying with her sister who is ill.'

'Surely her husband should come first?'

'She told him to come here and spend it with us and Jonathan.' Millie watched the game play out.

'So, she knows that Jacques is Jeremy's father?'

'Yes, she does. Jacques told her after Jonathan was born.' Millie frowned at Prue. 'Why all the questions?'

'It seems odd that his wife wouldn't come here for Christmas, that's all, especially with the baby.'

Monty leaned forward to place his final card. 'Perhaps Monsieur Baudin's wife wanted to stay with her sister, if the end is near?'

'Then he should be with his wife,' Cece put in.

Mama played her final card and won the game. 'And perhaps it is none of our business,' she whispered.

While the foursome played another hand, Millie went back over to the fireplace. Jeremy had left the room to get more wine and Grandmama was nodding in her chair.

Jacques gave Millie a gentle smile. 'I would ask a favour of you, *mon cher*?'

'Yes, of course.'

Jacques stared down at the flames, stroking his short beard. 'Would I be able to read Camile's letters?'

Millie didn't expect that question. 'Oh, I… er, yes. I don't suppose why not.'

'Jeremy has read them?'

'Yes, he has. It was hard for him. He didn't sleep well that night. It was as though she'd come back from the dead. He was troubled by the thought that she was never truly happy in her life.'

Nodding, Jacques bent to place another piece of wood on the fire. 'I understand why he would think that, but it's not entirely true. She was happy, when she was younger, when I knew her. She was beautiful and elegant, and all the men wanted her. I loved her greatly.'

'I think Camile loved you, too.'

'To read her letters will break my heart, but my heart broke all those years ago and has never recovered, so the pain is familiar.'

'But you must love your wife? You've had a long marriage to her.'

'*Oui*, we love each other, but it is not the great passion I had for Camile, and my wife has lived with that for our whole marriage. To my shame I could never make her feel she was just as worthy.' He continued squatting before the fire, staring into the flames. 'My wife and I have lived separate lives for years. There is a distance between us, more so since I told her about Jeremy.'

Millie felt sorry for her father-in-law. 'And what will reading Camile's letters achieve?'

He looked up at her, his eyes glazed with tears. 'For a short time, I will hear her voice and feel her touch. It is all I have left, and my memories of our short time together.'

'That's not true.' Millie put her hand on Jacques' shoulder. 'You have Jeremy and Jonathan and me. We are your family.'

'And that makes me a very happy man.' He smiled but the shadows of the past showed in his eyes.

Jeremy entered the room carrying bottles of wine. 'I had a thought while I was selecting what wine we should drink.'

'Oh?' Millie inquired.

'As lord and lady of Chateau Dumont it is our duty to show compassion to the whole region, along with other principle estates in the area.'

'Yes, I know.' Millie frowned. 'We do a great deal for people, Jeremy. We employ a good number of local staff, we have donated money to rebuild damaged buildings in the village, we are both on several committees to benefit the local community, both here in France and back in Yorkshire. What more can we possibly do?' She thought if she became any busier she'd die of exhaustion.

'We can always do more.'

'Such as?'

'I thought we could visit Épernay in the morning and take some food to hand out to people living in shelters. The cold weather is only making it worse for those who have returned to this area and have nothing,' Jeremy answered.

He let out a deep breath. 'I can't in good conscience attend a ball tomorrow night in Épernay knowing there are cold and starving people just a few hundred yards from where we are being lavishly entertained.'

'What food do you want to take and how much? We have our own family and staff to feed, remember.'

Jeremy looked at her in dismay. 'What, so you think we might starve if we only have three courses for dinner instead of seven? That we can't live on toast for breakfast instead of salmon?'

'That's not fair.' Millie was furious at him for making her sound selfish in front of everyone.

'*Mon fils.*' Jacques stood and put his hand on Jeremy's shoulder.

Jeremy shrugged his hand away. 'I am not *your* son. I am no one's son.'

Jacques raised his hands up in the French way, looking pained. 'The war has been over for two years. People are getting help from the government. It's not up to you to save everyone.'

'What do you know about it? You live in Paris. You don't face any hardships like the people here do.'

The raised voices drew the others from the card table.

Mama's eyebrows drew together in concern. 'What is the problem?'

'There is no problem, Mama,' Millie hurriedly assured her.

Jeremy swore under his breath.

'Well, I think it is a splendid idea,' Cece announced to the room. 'And I for one will help you distribute the food, Jeremy.'

Prue groaned. 'Must you always be a good little mouse?'

'How am I?' Cece defended. 'I wish to help the poor just as we do back in York. Unlike you, I'd rather do that than go shopping!'

'Of course, you would,' Prue murmured. She looked to Monty. 'What about you, Monty?'

He nodded. 'I will help.'

Cece preened. 'See, Prue? Not everyone is as selfish as you.'

'Shut up, Cece.'

'Enough, girls!' Mama gave a brittle smile. 'We will all go. This is Jeremy's home and if he wishes for us to help him feed the needy, then we shall.'

Millie, feeling unjustly side-lined, headed for the door. 'I'm going to bed. Goodnight all.'

Upstairs, she checked on Jonathan and found him fast asleep, as was his nurse who slept in the same room as him. She lingered for a long time, watching him breathing and trying to calm her own feelings.

When at last she went into her bedroom, Jeremy was already waiting for her. She glanced around for Royston, Jeremy's valet.

'I've sent Royston back to his cottage.'

She didn't reply.

'I'm sorry.' The contrite expression on his face showed her he was sincere. 'I was a rude bore to you and you know how much it hurts me when I speak so snappishly, especially to you, as I don't mean it. Sometimes I can't control myself.'

Millie went to the dressing table and took off her pearl necklace and earrings. 'I am not your enemy.'

'I know, my darling.' He stood behind her and wrapped his arms around her waist.

In the mirror he spoke to her. 'Sometimes, I can't control my thoughts. My temper is because I feel incapable... I speak too rashly. I'm impatient. I get frustrated too easily, particularly when it is to do with the war.'

'And I bear the brunt of it.' Millie moved out of his arms and slipped off her shoes.

'You do, yes, and I'm wish it wasn't so hard for you.'

She turned her back on him. 'I deal with your nightmares and I support you when something reminds you of the horrors of fighting in the war, but I will not be made to look a fool in front of my own family. That's not fair, Jeremy, and you know it.'

He hung his head. 'I'm sorry. Hurting you is the last thing I ever want to do.'

She gave him a cool look. 'You understand that I would gladly go with you and give out food.'

'Yes, I know.'

'But I have responsibilities here, too. As mistress of this house I also have to think of the food we have to feed the people directly under our care.

Vivian and the girls in the kitchen have been cooking for weeks, knowing we'd have guests for nearly a month.

You saw the amount of produce we had sent here from Paris, and yes, we can spare some of it, but Jacques is also correct.

You cannot save everyone. Those people aren't your soldiers. You are not responsible for them. You can no longer think as an army officer.'

'But I fought in a war that destroyed their homes, their towns, their livelihoods…'

'As did millions of other men, on both sides! You're not accountable for the whole damn war, Jeremy!' She was tired, so very tired of living with his guilty conscience.

Silence stretched between them.

'You are right, of course.' He sighed and sat on the edge of the bed. 'When I was receiving treatment in Plymouth, the doctors said part of suffering from shell shock is admitting to yourself that you aren't responsible for everything that happened in the war. What we did and what we saw was orchestrated by others. It is easier to say than do, but I am trying.'

She went and stood in front of him. 'I am not saying that we shouldn't help where we can, but you mustn't expect us to fix it all. You don't have to take that burden.'

He nodded. 'You're right.'

'You hurt Jacques tonight by saying you aren't his son.' Millie shook her head slightly. 'That is not the man I married.'

Jeremy ran a hand through his brown hair. 'I will apologise to him in the morning.'

'He is trying his best, too. None of this is easy for him. Yes, he didn't raise you, but that's not his fault, he didn't know about you. To blame him for all that happened to your mother is not right, or fair.'

'I'm trying not to blame him, Millie, really I am, but it's difficult. I just see her suffering being married to Soames, living in cold Remington Court when she could have been in Paris with Jacques.'

'But it was her choice. She made that decision, not Jacques. To blame him is unjust.'

'As I said, I will apologise to him in the morning.'

'He told me tonight that his marriage is over.'

Jeremy's eyes widened. 'I didn't know.'

'He feels he has failed in many ways; with Camile and you, and now his marriage. He wants to read Camile's letters. I said he could. It might help him in some way.'

'I will take them to him now. He was still sitting before the fire when I came up.'

'Will you unzip me first, please?' She turned her back to him to reach the zipper. She missed having Daisy, her maid who had come to France with her to do such things, but Daisy was married to Royston and pregnant and no longer her maid.

Once Jeremy had unzipped her dress and taken the pile of letters, he paused by the door. 'Do you forgive me?'

'Yes. But remember, you are not the only who suffers from the past. Everyone, in their own way, has their own battles to overcome.'

Chapter Four

In the grey light of a cold day, when the snow-heavy sky seemed so low you could touch it, Prue followed Jeremy and the others from the motor cars that had transported them into Épernay. Royston had driven the truck, which was filled with wooden crates of food raided from the chateau's larder. Jeremy had also gone to the village shops and bought what he could to add to the haul.

A layer of snow crunched under Prue's feet and her breath came out in puffs of vapour as she breathed. She hated the cold. She needed to live in a warm climate as freezing temperatures just made her cranky and snappy and she'd much rather spend her life laughing in the sun.

Jeremy led the family into a disused warehouse on the edge of town where he knew families had taken up residency for the winter while they waited for their homes to be rebuilt.

The bitter temperature made Prue snuggle down into the fur collar of her long blue coat, and, despite wearing gloves and boots, she couldn't feel her fingers and toes.

Inside the building, muted voices reached her and what seemed like a hundred pair of eyes stared.

Pity filled her at the sight of the makeshift homes of these people. Thin children sat on cold floors playing, while mothers hung washing that would never dry in this icy weather. Men lolled about, trying to keep pitiful fires burning or retying tarpaulins to stop them from falling down. Industry was going on though and she watched one man whittling wood to make a pipe, while another was mending a broken wooden chair. Many of the old women were knitting or sewing and Prue could feel the community vibe.

Jeremy went to one man and spoke in rapid French to him and his family. Prue couldn't completely understand what they were saying but no doubt Jeremy was explaining their mission. He beckoned Millie and the others to join him and soon word spread throughout the cavernous warehouse that *'les Anglais'* had brought food.

Royston and Monty started to unload the truck, and Prue collected a basket of vegetables. Filtering out amongst the people and their belongings, Prue stopped before a tent of tarpaulin and bowed her head to the woman with a child on her hip. 'Bonjour.'

'Bonjour,' the woman replied with a smile. Around her a gaggle of small children all chorused bonjour as well.

Prue's heart melted at the sight of them. She handed the mother a bunch of carrots and some onions. She wished she could give more but there were more people than food and it had to be shared out amongst them all.

Within minutes, she'd emptied her basket and returned to the truck.

'That was quick, miss.' Royston gave her another basket. 'We'll be out very quickly at this rate.'

'But it's so sad, Royston. That they have to live like this.'

He nodded. 'That's what war does to people. The innocent always suffer.'

'But to live in a chilly warehouse. Why don't they have the huts the government have built for other people? I've seen them on the side of the road.'

'Not everyone meets the requirements. Government rules and regulations and paperwork take time. There are so many displaced people. It'll take years to sort it out.'

'What we are doing feels so inadequate.'

'But at least we are doing something, miss.' Royston gave a grim smile.

Prue went along a different aisle and noticed Jacques helping Mama and Grandmama as they distributed loaves of bread.

Grandmama, who spoke better French than Prue, was chatting away to an old man who sat on a stool with a rug over his knees and a pipe hanging out of his mouth.

Young or old, rich or poor, her grandmother could talk to anyone and Prue was determined to be more like her. At least, do it in a fun style like Grandmama and not in the saintly style of Cece.

She glanced at Cece in another aisle standing close to Monty and sighed. Her sister was not in the least subtle when it came to showing her feelings over Monty. The poor man had made no promises to Cece, despite their exchange of letters for months. She doubted he was ever going to be serious in his intentions. Cece was making a fool of herself.

Quickly giving out her basket of vegetables to an elderly couple, Prue walked over to Cece and pulled her away from Monty. 'I think you should come and help me, Monty is more than capable of doing this row on his own.'

Cece jerked her arm free. 'Monty is helping me as I had a heavy box of potatoes,' she hissed. 'Go away.'

'I'll not stand by and watch you make a fool of yourself over him.'

'Be quiet.'

'I will not,' Prue whispered, frustrated with her stubborn sister. 'At every opportunity you're making cow eyes at him. It's embarrassing.'

'You know nothing!'

Prue softened her tone. 'I'm worried about you, that's all. You are obsessed with him.'

'Don't be ridiculous. We are friends.'

'You want more than friendship.'

'And who is to say I can't have that? *You*?' Cece snapped. 'Stay out of it, Prue. It's not my fault you don't have *anyone*!'

Hurt and anger rose in Prue's chest. 'Fine, have it your way. But don't come crying to me when he throws you to one side. He obviously doesn't want you, and even though he carries scars, he's still not desperate enough to settle for you!'

'Girls!' Mama stood behind them, the thin tight line of her mouth showing her displeasure. 'Why do you both still act like children? Did I not have enough of this behavior when you were growing up? I think we should head back to the motor cars. *Now*.' She turned on her heel and they knew to follow.

'I'll not forgive you for what you just said,' Cece whispered angrily.

'Good. I don't want you to, as I'm not forgiving you,' Prue muttered.

Back at the motor cars, Prue headed for Jacques smart little green sports car.

'No, Prue.' Mama halted her. 'I'm travelling back with Jacques, you are to go with Millie, Jeremy and Grandmama.'

'What about Monty?'

'He's travelling with Cece and Royston in the truck.'

Fuming, Prue stormed in the direction of Jeremy's Fiat, but her step faltered as Mama smiled and chuckled at something Jacques said to her.

Her heart missed a beat at the way Mama tilted her head a little to give Jacques her full attention. Was her mother *flirting*?

She hurried over to Cece who was sat up in the truck and opened the door.

'Go away, Prue!' Cece reached to close the door again.

'Be quiet and listen.' Prue scowled at her. 'Did you see Mama and Jacques just now?'

Cece squinted through the dirty windscreen. 'No, why?'

'Mama was flirting with him!'

'No!' Cece inhaled sharply. 'You're mistaken, Mama wouldn't. She couldn't.'

That statement irritated Prue. 'Why couldn't she, for God's sake? She's a woman being flattered by a handsome man. She's not made of stone.'

'She's our mother!'

'So?'

Cece struggled for words. 'Papa hasn't been gone a year yet!'

'Does that matter? He will be soon, in a couple of months. Mama is still here and living.' Prue studied her parent, and probably for the first time realised that their mother was still an attractive woman, tall, with a shapely figure and not a lot of grey in her black hair.

'It's not right,' Cece broke into her thoughts.

'Don't be such a prude.' Prue suddenly laughed. 'Imagine, if Mama married Jacques, that would make Millie and Jeremy brother and sister as well as husband and wife!'

'You're obscene!' Cece spat and slammed the door shut.

Prue laughed harder.

~ ~ ~ ~

Millie was swept around the Grand Salon of the Pol-Roger's establishment in Épernay in the arms of their host, Maurice Pol-Roger.

A debonair man, Maurice, alongside his brother George, were hosting the annual Christmas party for the champagne growers in the North of France.

This was the first one she'd attended and was so pleased when the brothers included her family to join them on the invitation.

Reluctantly, Grandmama had stayed home dealing with a headache.

However, Jacques and Mama, Prue, Cece and Monty had dressed in their finest and were now mixing amongst some of the most important families of France, or at least in the champagne world.

When the music finished, Maurice bowed to Millie. *'Merci, Madame Remington.'*

'Merci, monsieur.' She smiled, happy that Jeremy came to claim her for the next dance.

As the music swelled again, they moved in time.

Jeremy leaned closer to her ear. 'Have I told you how beautiful you look tonight?'

'You have but I always want to hear it again.' She was pleased she'd worn a new dress of soft rose pink that shimmered in the light. From the drop waist a tasseled hem reached down to just below her knees. At Prue's insistence she'd worn white feathers in her curls that contrasted well against her dark hair.

'Well, you do. Every man here is interested to know who is Millie, Lady Remington from Chateau Dumont.'

'Really?' She laughed, not believing him for a second.

'Oh yes, and with Jacques and Monty parading your mother and sisters around the dance floor, the *new blood* is causing a stir. Many of the *houses* are wanting to talk to me and Jacques tonight.'

'How interesting.'

'Yes, after the holidays I'm meeting with the heads of some important houses, Perrier-Jouët, Moët and Chandon and Boizel, amongst others, to let them know I'm serious in creating superior champagne, and of being a part of the industry in this region. It's my heritage.'

'Are we here to dance or to do business?' she asked, with a saucy lift of one of her eyebrows. She knew once he started talking about the business he'd not stop.

'Both, my darling,' his lips whispered against her cheek. 'We are looking to expand the business. I want Chateau Dumont champagne to be in every country in the world.'

'Big plans.'

'I can do it, Millie.' He pulled back to stare into her eyes. 'I *will* do it.'

She squeezed his hand. 'I know you can and will, my love. Between you and Jacques, you'll make the estate grow.'

'We need to employ more managers, to export, and have offices in other countries.'

'Even though the markets to Russia and America are closed?'

'There are other countries in the world and in ten years' time I predict that both Russia and America will be drinking our champagne, despite their laws.'

'And what about what Grandmama said about filling French restaurants with our champagne?'

'Consider it done, or at least in the planning stage. Jacques and I will ramp up the marketing in that area, and then I believe, with more agents out there spreading the word, we can ride through this tough time.'

They swirled around some other couples, and Millie noted that Jacques was partnering Mama yet again.

'Darling?' Jeremy raised an eyebrow. 'Are you listening to me?'

'Hmm?' She didn't really want to talk business tonight. Tonight, was for dancing, drinking, and enjoying herself away from the responsibilities of running a chateau.

'I want to employ Monty to run an office in London.'

Her step faltered, but Jeremy held her and glided them along. 'Monty in London? What about his role at Remington Court?'

'We both know he is capable of far better things than running a country estate. With his education and contacts, I feel he'd make a better manager of our London office.'

'I see.'

The music stopped, and they walked to a secluded corner of the room.

Jeremy frowned. 'You aren't in agreement?'

'What about Remington Court?'

'I want to try to sell it.' Jeremy pulled at his white collar.

'Sell it?'

'I've never liked the place and well… since I'm not really a Remington, I'd rather get shot of it all, and the memories it holds.'

'But you said yourself only months ago that no one wants to buy country estates these days. They are too expensive to run.'

'I know. That's why I'm thinking of advertising it in America, where the money is. I feel if we can sell Remington Court, then we can use that money to expand the selling of our champagne around the world.

It's a far better future for us than holding onto Remington Court. Unless you wish to go back and live there?'

Millie shook her head. 'No, not at all. It holds no nice memories for me, either. You left me there alone for months while you were in Plymouth and I lost our first baby there.' She shuddered. 'No, I have no intention of going back. When we are in Yorkshire to visit my family, we can stay with Mama, and we have the townhouse in Kensington.'

'They were my thoughts also.'

'France and the chateau are our home, the place we'll raise our children. I'm happy with that.'

He kissed her soundly and smiled. 'Children? We've only just had one.'

She cupped his cheek. 'We can't let Jonathan be an only child.'

A devilish desire sparked in his eyes. 'Shall we try tonight then, wife?'

She laughed and gently slapped him away. 'Perhaps in the New Year. I'd like to have my figure back for a few more months yet, please.'

'What are you two doing hiding in the corner?' Prue asked, smiling and hanging on the arm of an eager young man. 'This is Phillipe, I've forgotten his surname, not that it matters, but we are heading to the refreshments table. Care to join us?'

'Millie, Prue!' Cece suddenly appeared from nowhere, yelling for them.

'What is it?' Millie demanded. Cece's white face made Millie's heart sink.

'It's Mama, she's suffered a bad turn or something. Come quickly!' She turned and fled back into the crowd.

Millie and the others followed, pushing and excusing themselves through the dancers and guests until they were in a hallway and hurrying down it.

'Where is she?' Millie asked.

'Jacques and some other man who is a doctor took her in here.' Cece ran into a large room with wooden panelling and shelves of books that must be a study or library.

Mama was laying on a chaise-longue with a stranger kneeling next to her and Jacques hovering by her head.

'Mama?' Millie rushed to her side.

The man, doctor, spoke in French and Jeremy translated. 'She's doing fine now. Her pulse is racing, and she's overheated.'

'I'm perfectly fine,' Mama murmured, her face pale. 'I simply fainted, too hot with all that dancing.'

'You've not stopped all night!' Cece took her to task. 'You've danced more than any of us. Jacques, I'm blaming you!'

'Be quiet, Cece,' Mama said, trying to sit up. 'I was having a lovely time. Surely that is allowed?'

The doctor helped her upright and gave her a glass of water to sip. '*Comment vous sentez-vous?*'

Mama, knowing some French, smiled a little. 'I'm perfectly well now, merci.'

'I think we should go home,' Millie said. They'd only lost their father ten months ago and the shock of that still affected them all.

'No, Millie, I'm fine. It will ruin the night.'

'Mama, we've been here hours,' Prue added. 'You are more important than a party. Let us go.'

Within minutes they were taking their leave and saying goodbye to their hosts and the new acquaintances they'd made.

Splitting up into two motor cars, they made the silent drive back to the chateau. Once inside, Millie, Prue and Cece assisted Mama into bed. Grandmama slept in the bed at the opposite side of the room and they tried to be as quiet as they could.

'You're making too much fuss, girls,' Mama complained quietly as they aided her in undressing and putting on her nightgown.

'What is going on?' Grandmama mumbled from the other bed. 'Why can't a person get any sleep?'

'Mama had a bad turn, Grandmama,' Cece whispered.

'Stop whispering, child. I can't hear a word you're saying!'

Cece went closer to Grandmama's bed. 'We brought Mama home, she wasn't well.'

Grandmama struggled to sit up and when she did, she peered at her daughter.

'Violet! What is this nonsense? What does Cece mean you aren't well? You're never sick.'

'It's all right, Mother. I fainted from the heat while dancing. Silly of me really.'

'Fainted?' Grandmama frowned. 'Turn the lamp up, Cece, I can't see a damn thing.'

Cece quickly lit the lamp beside the bed.

Grandmama glowered. 'Fainting from dancing? How ridiculous! What are you, an old maid?'

'Well, no, but I'm not entirely young either, Mother.'

'Don't talk rubbish. I'm old, you are not.'

'I'm fifty.'

'I know what age you are, didn't I give birth to you?'

Mama pulled the blankets over her neatly. 'All I'm saying is that I'm not twenty, and perhaps I was dancing a little too much for my age.'

'Tosh! Fifty, what age is that, I beg!' Grandmama glared at them all. 'I've never fainted in my life, and I could dance all night if I wanted too.'

'Then why didn't you come with us, Grandmama?' Prue teased.

'Because I had a slight headache and I wanted a night to myself without you all bothering me, that's why. And don't be saucy with me, girl!

Now get out the lot of you and let me sleep,' Grandmama grumbled and nestled back down on her pillows. 'A member of my family fainting. How weak. Disgraceful behaviour.'

Millie ushered her sisters out of the bedroom and once they were in the galley, they hid their giggles behind their hands.

'We shouldn't laugh,' Cece said.

'But it's funny,' Prue chuckled. 'Grandmama will tear strips off Mama in the morning for embarrassing the family.'

'It's hardly Mama's fault,' Millie said. 'Anyone can faint in a hot room. There was no air in there, just hot bodies all squashed together.'

Cece became serious. 'Jacques shouldn't have danced with her so much. She's still in mourning.'

Prue gave her a side look. 'Be quiet, you killjoy. Mama can dance as much as she likes, we aren't Victorian. She has grieved terribly over Papa, but she is allowed to be happy, too.'

'But not with him!' Cece hissed.

Millie frowned. 'Why not with Jacques?'

Prue grinned. 'Cece doesn't want Mama and Jacques becoming an item.'

'What would make you think that they are?' Millie was confused.

'Haven't you noticed how much time they spend together?' Cece scoffed. 'It's not right.'

'We are all living together, of course they'll spend time together over Christmas.'

'Cece is worried Mama will fall for Jacques. He is, after all, a good-looking man,' Prue said.

'Mama is still mourning Papa, and Jacques is married.' Even as Millie said the words, she knew they sounded ineffectual. She knew Jacques wasn't in love with his wife and they were all but separated in every way but name. 'I'm going to bed, and you both should not think too deeply about this. It's not going to happen. Mama's life is in York and Jacques is in Paris.'

'I'd be happy to live in Paris!' Prue's eyes lit up.

'Do shut up!' Cece stormed off into their bedroom.

Millie gave Prue a quelling look. 'Don't stir her up, please. It's Christmas Eve tomorrow. Let us have a nice day.'

Prue raised her hands in surrender. 'I won't, but she's acting like a child.'

Chapter Five

Millie sat in the rocking chair in the corner of the nursery and held Jonathan in her arms. A cheery fire crackled in the small fireplace and from the incubator came a soft bubbling of the boiler heating up the water. Outside on the chateau's front lawn, she could hear the squeals of Cece, Prue and Monty having a snowball fight. Jonathan had finished feeding and was content to stare at her with an interested expression on his face.

Mille grinned. 'What are you thinking, little man?' She stroked his soft cheek with a finger. 'Do you know that this time next year, you'll be probably walking and getting into mischief? You'll be able to rip off the wrapping on your presents and have enormous fun.'

A knock on the open door made her look up. 'Come in,' she told Jacques.

'I do not wish to disturb you, *mon cher*.'

'No, we are finished, and this little man has a full tummy. I'm just enjoying a quiet cuddle with him while Nursé Allard has gone to Paris for the day to see her family for Christmas.'

'Ah, Jeremy and Royston took her to the train station this morning, *oui?*'

'Oui.'

'I have come to ask for a pair of Jonathan's shoes.'

'Jonathan? He doesn't have any shoes, he's far too little.' She grinned.

Jacques shook his head with a smile. 'Socks, perhaps?'

'Here, hold him.' Millie passed the baby over and went to the white armoire. She looked through the drawers and found a selection of knitted booties. 'Will these do?'

'*Oui, merci.*'

'Why do you want them?'

'French tradition. Children's shoes are filled with carrots and treats for *Père Noël's* donkey.'

'Father Christmas has a donkey?'

Jacques nodded seriously. '*Oui.* Jonathan must do this as a child in France at Christmas.'

'All right.' She handed them over. 'It is only right that we keep traditions alive, both English and French.'

'Important, *oui.*'

Millie watched Jacques gaze down at the baby. 'I am happy that Jonathan will have a grandfather in his life, since my own father is no longer with us.'

'I will cherish him. I'm honoured to be a *grand-père*. With Jonathan I get to be someone, finally.'

'You are more than just a grandfather, Jacques, you are a father, too.'

'I do not know so much…'

'Time will help with Jeremy. There is much he has to deal with. His shell shock, although better since living here at the chateau, still plagues him.

There have been nights where he has yelled in his sleep calling for his mother to help him save the men he was fighting with during the war. His dreams are getting all mixed up now. Before it was just the war and the men who died beside him. But since we found Camile's letters, and he became aware of his true parentage, he's had much more on his mind. Then, there are the concerns with the business to add to his worries. He's finding it tough.'

'I know he struggles.'

'All I'm saying is that you mustn't give up on him.'

'Non, but Jeremy is a grown man. I knew him only as a friend, he is my employer. Now, all is so complicated…'

'The business is a common bond you share, that can be built upon and in time you can become more father and son.'

Jacques shrugged one shoulder, clearly not believing her. 'We've all read Camile's letters. She needed me, and I wasn't there.'

'She never told you she was pregnant.'

'Non. I wish she had.'

Millie hesitated to bring up another delicate matter, but she needed to know. 'There is something I would like to ask you?'

'Oui?'

'I wondered what you thought of my mother.'

Jacques frowned, his mouth turned down. 'I do not understand.'

'My sisters believe you have... intentions regarding Mama.'

He looked back down at the baby who was now asleep. 'Violet is a beautiful woman. She is lonely, as am I. We enjoy one another's company. Is that a bad thing?'

'No, but she is still in mourning for our father.'

'*Oui.*'

'And you are married.'

'It is only a formality,' he said sadly.

'Then you do want a relationship with Mama?'

He opened the incubator door and carefully placed Jonathan inside it and closed the door before turning to Millie. 'I do not know what the future will hold, *mon cher*. Your mama is her own woman. When I am free, I will write to her and see what she says. Until then, we are friends.'

'I see.'

'I admire your mama, but life is not simple. I am a busy man, and Jeremy wants to expand. However, I am not getting any younger and I wish to be happy.'

'Everyone deserves to be happy.'

'After reading Camile's letters I know that we both wasted a lifetime together. Everything would have been so different if we'd been brave enough to go after what we wanted. I do not want to make that same mistake again.' He gave her a small smile, but his sad expression spoke to her more than his words.

Millie realised that this man had worked hard all his life to export Chateau Dumont's champagne while in a loveless marriage. He deserved some happiness. She impulsively reached up and kissed his cheek. 'I am happy to call you my father-in-law, and for my son to have you as a grandfather.'

'Shall we go open a bottle of champagne?' He raised an eyebrow in question.

'I think that is a perfect idea.'

With a last check on Jonathan, they left the nursery and crossed the gallery to the stairs. As they were descending, the front door opened and Monty, Cece and Prue came in laughing and covered in snow.

'Good Lord, you must be freezing!' Millie said. 'Go and get changed. We are having some champagne before the meal starts.'

'I'm looking forward to it, I'm starving,' Prue announced, heading up the stairs.

'I shall just check on how Vivian is coping,' Millie said as Jacques headed through a door and down into the cellars.

In the kitchen, Vivian and her girls, Catrin and Sophie, were occupied with several tasks at once as they toiled to create a splendid feast. Delightful aromas filled the air and the heat from the cooking ranges was intense. Millie was surprised to see Daisy sitting at the huge pine table shelling walnuts. 'Daisy, how are you feeling?'

'Fat, madam, very fat.'

'Oh dear, and you've still got a couple of months to go,' Millie joked.

Daisy blushed and glanced away. 'I've come to help Vivian and the girls. I'm bored sitting in the cottage by myself. At least I can sit and cut up begetables.'

'When is Royston due back?'

'I don't know. He and Sir Jeremy went to Reims after dropping off Nursé Allard at the station this morning.'

'Yes, Jeremy did mention something about that this morning, but I was half asleep and didn't fully take it in.'

Daisy flinched as she reached for more walnuts.

'Are you feeling all right, Daisy?' Millie asked, concerned.

'Yes, thank you, madam. I just think the baby is sitting funny.'

Millie nodded. 'They tend to do that. Jonathan used to kick me so hard.' She turned to Vivian. 'All is well in here?'

'*Oui, madame.*' Vivian wiped her forehead with her arm. She looked tired as she scooped out creamy potatoes from a large pan into a tureen.

'You and the girls are to go home afterwards and not come back until tomorrow evening. We can manage by ourselves during the day tomorrow.'

'*Non, madame*, it is Christmas Day. How will you cope?'

'We'll have enough food left over from today's meal to feed us tomorrow. I insist, Vivian. You and the girls have worked so hard, and I want you all to have time with your families.'

'I can help, madam,' Daisy said. 'I can cook breakfast in the morning.'

'No, Daisy. I'll not have you exhausted as well. You're meant to be taking it easy.'

'Oh, I'll be fine. Besides, Royston is always out and about with Sir Jeremy and I get bored at the cottage by myself. That's why I spend so much time in this kitchen, I hate being on my own.'

'As long as you're sure?'

'I am.'

'Then, thank you. You'll get help from me and my sisters in the morning.'

'Good luck getting Miss Prue out of bed in time.' Daisy chuckled. 'I remember how she used to be, not one for early rising.'

'True.' Millie had a thought. 'Would you mind sitting with Jonathan while his nurse is away today?'

Daisy heaved herself up. 'I would like that a lot. I'll go up now.'

'Thank you, it'll free up some of my time.'

Vivian opened the oven door and took out a tray of chicken pieces. '*Le réveillon de Noël* to start in one hour?'

'Oui, that would be perfect. I'll gather my family into the dining room in an hour.'

Millie left the kitchen and headed for the Grand Salon. There she found Grandmama sitting alone. 'Where is everyone?'

'Getting changed I should imagine.' Grandmama put down the newspaper she was reading and gave Millie the once over. 'Are you not changing?'

Millie glanced down at her navy blue dress with its satin sleeves and skirt. 'No, I'm not. Jonathan will want feeding when we are eating and I'm not getting changed to then change again.'

'Put the child on a bottle, for heaven's sake. You've got a nanny, make her do her job.'

'You know I'm feeding him myself because he was so tiny. It's worked and look how well he is doing. He'll start bottle feeding soon enough, anyway, when in the spring I take up my duties again as mistress of this chateau and all that involves.'

'Children have survived not being fed from their mother's breast. Don't be a martyr.'

'I'm not. Anyway, I'm sorry, but I'm not getting dressed for dinner.' Millie had never been so defiant to her grandmama in her life.

Grandmama's eyes widened. 'To not get dressed for dinner? What is this? A revolution? Have you become entirely French now and will do as you please? Next you'll do away with the minimal staff you have and serve us yourself!'

'That's exactly what I plan to do tomorrow.' Millie beamed.

'You are what?' Grandmama threw the newspaper down. 'Outrageous behaviour. I do not know what is becoming of this family, really I don't. You are Lady Remington, not a farmer's wife. The world has gone completely mad.'

'It's the modern ways, Grandmama. The war changed everything. We have more freedom to do as we like, we can bend the rules.'

'Bend the rules! Good God, girl, I broke enough of them in my time, but there still needs to be a sense of doing things the correct way. At this rate Jonathan will grow up as wild as a native Indian.'

'Well, I can assure you he won't be sent off to boarding school as a young boy as Jeremy was.'

Grandmama scoffed. 'There's nothing wrong with toughening them up, girl. Boarding schools make them men. Look at Jeremy, a war hero.'

Before Millie could reply that real war heroes suffer more than most, Mama, Prue and Cece entered the room.

Prue went straight to the drinks' cabinet. 'What is this meal, then Millie?'

'It's a French tradition.'

'Oh, you're happy to support a *French* tradition then!' Grandmama sniffed.

Millie ignored her. 'Jacques says on Christmas Eve French people have a large and very long meal throughout the afternoon and evening. It's a time for family to all come together.'

'Well, we are British, and we've been together for weeks already,' Grandmama mumbled.

They heard a commotion at the door and Jeremy walked in and with him was Stephen Isaacs, his best friend.

'Stephen!' Millie embraced him warmly. 'This is a lovely surprise. I didn't know you were in France.'

'Yes, I've been deployed with my men to help with the search and recovery of missing soldiers,' he said sadly. 'There are still a great many unaccounted for.'

Millie squeezed his hands. 'A noble task indeed.'

'You don't mind me staying for Christmas, Lady Rem?' he asked cheekily.

'Not in the slightest. How wonderful! You know everyone except Jacques. He'll be down in a minute.'

'I've heard a lot about him.' Stephen shook hands with everyone.

Millie tucked her arm through Jeremy's. 'How did this come about?'

'Stephen sent a telegram to us this morning, I happened to get it when I was in Épernay dropping Nursé Allard off at the train station. Monsieur Bosse from the post office saw me cross the street, and gave it to me in person, which was a stroke of luck, as Royston and I were heading to Reims anyway, and that's where Stephen was.'

'Why were you going to Reims?'

Jeremy kissed her cheek. 'To look at a new grape press that I heard was available. I did tell you. Anyway, it survived the bombings somehow but the viner —'

'Did you buy it?' Jacques asked coming into the room with Monty and hearing the last bit of the conversation.

'I did indeed. Having another press will increase output. It's on the back of the truck now. Pascal and Royston are inspecting it, but I thought to bring Stephen in and meet the family and I need to change. Stephen's not interested in the making of champagne.'

Stephen laughed. 'No, only the drinking of it!'

'Hear! Hear!' Prue chorused.

Vivian appeared in the doorway and gave Millie a nod to indicate the meal was ready to start.

'Let us all be going into the dining room,' Millie announced. 'Le réveillon de Noël is about to start.'

'Is that some kind of Christmas dinner?' Stephen asked, escorting Mama across the hall.

'I believe so,' she replied. 'A feast, apparently. You have great timing, Mr Isaacs.'

He winked. 'I always have, Mrs Marsh, I always have.'

An extra place setting was arranged for Stephen while Jeremy raced upstairs to change.

'I say Mrs Fordham, you become more beautiful every time I see you,' Stephen said to Grandmama.

'Does such smooth talk get you anywhere with the ladies, Mr Isaacs?'

He grinned. 'Not always, Mrs Fordham.'

'Then come sit by me and flatter me some more, and I'll advise you on where you are going wrong.'

General hilarity filled the room as Stephen flirted with Grandmama. Candelabras centred down the long table gave a golden glow, adding to the soft electric lights on the walls. Sprigs of evergreen were draped along the mantelpiece and scented apple wood burned in the fire giving off a scent of the outdoors.

When everyone was seated, and Jeremy returned to pour the champagne, Catrin and Sophie began serving the first course of foie gras and slivers of toast.

From the corner of her eye, Millie saw Nursé Allard walk by and was shocked. The nanny wasn't meant to be back until tomorrow.

Excusing herself, Millie went out into the hallway and halted the woman before she went upstairs. 'Nursé Allard? You are back early.'

'*Oui, madame.*' The woman looked as though she had been crying.

'Whatever is the matter?'

'My family I was to have stayed with have gone away and didn't tell me.' Tears filled her eyes and she wiped them away. 'I thought there was no point of me staying in Paris alone. I came back. You do not mind, *madame?*'

'No, of course not.' Millie felt sorry for the older woman. To have no member of her family with her at Christmas must be terribly upsetting. 'It is not good that your family didn't tell you they were going away.'

'We are not close, not anymore.' Allard took a deep breath. 'I will spend the evening with Master Jonathan, at least I know he needs me.'

'Thank you.' Millie touched her arm affectionately. 'I will come up and feed him in a couple of hours. I'll have one of the girls bring you up a tray.'

'*Merci, madame.*'

Returning to the dining room, Millie told the table that the nurse was back and her unhappy plight.

'We must be thankful for what we have,' Jeremy said quietly, giving Millie a loving smile.

'To have no one would be dreadful, don't you think?' Prue sipped her champagne. 'I couldn't imagine it.'

Stephen rested his fork down. 'I know I'd rather be here than at the barracks we've been assigned to while we are in France. A most depressing place, indeed.'

'You're lucky you have some leave,' Millie said, finishing her *foie gras*.

'Luck has nothing to do with it, Lady Rem. I'm in charge on this mission and well… it's Christmas, why wouldn't I want to spend it at my best friend's chateau?' He grinned and raised his champagne flute in a toast. 'To family and friends.'

Everyone echoed his words, and then all started talking about the next course of lobster that Vivian had just carried into the room.

'Golly, I am going to be so fat!' Prue declared.

Monty shook his head. 'Not you. You've got the figure of a greyhound.'

Prue laughed. 'What a deep chest and spindly legs?'

As they laughed, Millie watched Cece. Her sister's smile didn't reach her eyes. Millie knew she hated it when Monty gave attention to Prue.

She sighed, wondering what on earth was going to come of Cece's infatuation.

They tucked into the serving of lobster with a thyme and cream sauce. Jeremy opened another bottle of champagne.

'Will we open presents tonight?' Prue asked.

'Certainly not!' Grandmama said. 'In this family presents are opened after church on Christmas Day.' She glared at Millie. 'Will you change that also?'

'No, Grandmama. Presents will be tomorrow.' Millie hid a smile, knowing that she'd pleased her grandmama at least once today.

Stephen coughed politely. 'You'll have to forgive me, as I've not brought presents. There was no preparation to shop for gifts, I apologise.'

'That's all right, Stephen,' Prue said, sipping her champagne. 'We've got none to give you either.'

He grinned and clinked his glass against hers. 'My being here should be a present enough I hope?'

Prue tilted her head and gazed at him from under her lashes. 'Perhaps, but only if you dance with me later.'

'What is that noise?' Mama suddenly asked.

Millie lifted her head, listening and just made out the sound of singing. 'Oh, it could be carolers.'

Prue clapped her hands. 'How wonderful. We must go out and watch them.'

In the midst of scrapping back chairs and excited talking, the food was forgotten as coats were sought.

Jeremy opened the tall front doors and spilled light out onto the steps and there, standing in the gently falling snow, were a dozen people from the nearby villages singing. From the oldest grey-whiskered man to a few young children with rosy cheeks, they held their song books in front of them and sung with gusto. They looked like a picture and Millie was enchanted by it.

'It sounds so lovely sung in French, doesn't it?' Cece said on a happy sigh.

Millie glanced at her family, content that on this special evening they were having a wonderful time. She noticed Jacques standing close to Mama, and that they were whispering. Millie looked away and caught Prue's eye. Prue had also seen the intimate exchange.

Millie concentrated on the singers. If Mama was to seek another man's company, then no one could stop her but as the image of her darling papa come to mind, Millie couldn't help but feel a little sad that so much was changing.

Chapter Six

Alone in the bedroom she shared with Prue, Cece held the present in her hands. The gift for Monty should be under the tree, but she didn't know the correct etiquette for giving non-members of the family presents. She knew Prue hadn't bought one for him, nor had Mama or Grandmama. Only Millie and Jeremy had a gift for him. However, she felt differently. Monty was the man she loved. She'd tried to fight it, but nothing she did or thought reduced her feelings for him. Today she would leave him in no doubt of her feelings. It was Christmas Day. Surely, he wouldn't spurn her today of all days?

She just had to time it right.

Leaving the room, she closed the door and jumped a little as Monty came out of his room along the gallery. She wasn't expecting to see him right now. 'Monty.' She was suddenly nervous.

'Cece.' His smile always made her weak at the knees. 'You've another present to add to the collection under the tree?'

'Yes, no.' She swallowed. 'This is for you.'

'For me?' His eyebrows rose.

'I hope you like it.'

'I didn't expect a present from anyone. I came with very little myself, mainly just a present for young Jonathan as Millie said that I wasn't expected to buy for the family.'

It hurt that he hadn't bought her a gift. She thought that she might mean a bit more to him than just as a member of Millie's family, after all, they had been writing letters to each other all year. 'Oh, well, it's just something I thought you might like. Just to show that... well... that I value our friendship.'

'I'm flattered. Shall I open it now?'

She nodded and walked to him, the present held out in front of her.

He took it from her and she gazed at his freshly shaven cheeks, even his scars on his jaw and neck didn't detract from his handsome face. He wore a soft grey suit and a white shirt with a dark grey tie. Her fingers itched to slide up into his slick-backed hair.

'Thank you for this.' He smiled, unwrapping the paper. 'It's very unexpected.'

She watched him reveal the dark leather briefcase with gold clasps.

'Wow, Cece. This is very generous.' He turned the briefcase over in his hands, inspecting it.

'It's handmade, and look, it has your initials on the top.' She blushed with joy at seeing how much he liked the gift.

'Thank you very much, but you shouldn't have gone to such expense and trouble.'

'I wanted to.' She looked up at his face, aching for him to kiss her. 'You mean a lot to me and I wanted to show you that.'

'Cece…' he chastised her gently. 'I've told you in our letters, I'm not ready to give you what you want.'

She glanced away, heartbroken. 'I don't want anything, but you,' she whispered.

'I'm in no position to be in any kind of relationship. I thought you understood that? I told you about my difficult past in my letters. I'm not ready.'

'Not ready for anyone or just me?'

'Cece, I like you, you know that.'

'I don't want to be liked, Monty. I want you to love me as I love you.'

'Don't. Don't say you love me.' He shook his head, backing away from her. He opened his bedroom door and went inside the room.

Impulsively, Cece followed him. 'You're walking away after I've just told you how much I care about you?'

'I'm trying to be fair to you.' He put the briefcase on the chair by the door. 'I work for your sister and brother-in-law. I have no more than the wage I earn and the cottage they provide me. I may be an earl's son, but that is all gone now.'

'If you're worried about money, I have my inheritance from Papa. We'll be fine. I can live simply.' She tried not to sound desperate, but she was.

'No.'

'Are you too proud to live off my money?

'Yes, yes I am!' he snapped. 'Naturally I would be.'

'Well, that's just nonsense, really it is!'

'Not to me. Granted there are many families now who have lost their wealth and are happy to marry into other families who are rich, but that is not me. I have nothing to offer you, at least not the luxury you expect.'

'I don't care about any of that, don't you see?'

He backed away from her and stuck his hands in his pockets. 'You've never lived simply, you wouldn't know how to do so. *I* know how it is, and it's difficult. I went from living in splendour to sleeping rough. I grew up with a house full of servants and now I take care of myself. Can you even imagine how difficult that is? You've not experienced it, you don't know.'

'I'm willing to try. Millie has done it here. This chateau is only half restored, and she manages just fine with hardly any servants. Jeremy is a baron, and he works in the vineyard alongside his workers.'

'Millie and Jeremy have money, they have *some* staff to help them. I've learned to cook for myself and build my own fire. I live in a small cottage on their estate, which has tiny cramped rooms, chimneys that smoke and windows which let in draughts.'

'So, we'll fix it up.'

She stepped closer to him and grabbed his arms, annoyed at his stubbornness.

Then she had a thought. 'You don't find me attractive, do you?'

'Cece...'

'I'm not beautiful like Prue, am I?'

'Yes, you're lovely in your own way.'

Her head dropped. She'd never stack up against Prue.

'Please, don't be upset.'

'How can I not be?' Her voice caught in her throat. 'The man I love doesn't love me. If I was as pretty as Prue you'd want me. Unless it is Prue you want?'

'Stop talking nonsense. I don't want Prue in the slightest. She is the last sister I would pick.'

Cece frowned in surprise. 'So, you'd pick *Millie* over me too?'

A crimson flush stole over Monty's face. 'You're twisting my words.'

Suddenly Cece saw what was right in front of her.

She thought back to all the times she was at Remington Court before Millie left there. The occasions when Monty bent over backwards to help Millie, to ease her difficult time while Jeremy was away receiving treatment for shell shock. He couldn't do enough for her, even though Millie didn't like him, blamed him for putting a wedge between her and Jeremy, and still Monty was devoted.

'Cece...'

'It's *Millie* you want.'

'No, no. She loves Jeremy.' He looked flustered.

'Yes, she does, but *you* love *her*.'

'No, I don't. I thought I might have done, maybe... I respect her, of course, but I wasn't sure —'

She took a step back, her stomach in knots. 'How silly of me.'

'Cece, stop this.'

'Tell me I'm wrong.' She glared at him, fighting the tears. 'Tell me you don't love Millie.'

'Of course, I admire her... she's...'

He didn't outright deny it and that was enough for Cece. 'I've made such a fool of myself, forgive me.'

'No, no, not at all. I'm flattered by your affection, truly. You do mean a lot to me.'

'But not enough.' She forced a weak smile to her face, doing her best to keep the last remaining bit of her dignity. 'I won't bother you again.' She turned and left the room.

Running back to her own bedroom, she shut the door and leaned against it as the tears flowed. 'Merry Christmas to me,' she whispered.

~ ~ ~ ~

Millie gave Jonathan back to Nursé Allard. 'That should keep him going for a little while.'

'*Madame* would like to give him the bottle later?'

Hesitating, Millie felt torn.

She enjoyed feeding Jonathan herself, but it was becoming tiring with a house full of guests and after the holidays she'd need to throw herself into finishing the chateau's renovations and begin to immerse herself in the surrounding villages.

As a chateau owner, she and Jeremy were responsible for many community charities, plus the champagne business was to be expanded and if that took Jeremy away, then she'd have to take over his role on the estate, which ultimately meant she'd have to learn more about growing grapes and making champagne.

'*Madame?*'

Millie sighed and nodded. 'Yes, give him the bottle.' She felt instantly guilty.

'*Oui, madame.*' Nursé Allard placed him in the incubator. 'Perhaps, *madame* thinks the incubator should go, too?'

'No!' Millie put her hands up in protest. 'He stays in the incubator. It's warm in there and although the fires are lit in all the rooms up here on this floor, the chateau is frightfully cold. He must be kept warm until he is bigger.'

'*Oui, madame.*' The other woman checked the boiler at the side of the incubator and satisfied it was as it should be, she set about clearing away the baby's dirty clothes.

Millie lingered, staring through the glass at her son.

He'd done better than anyone expected, and continued to grow, but the fear of having him so early still remained.

She looked at the nurse. 'You won't leave him.'

'*Non, madame.*' The older woman smiled warmly.

'I'll have a tray brought up for you mid-morning.'

Leaving the baby's room, Millie met Cece coming out of her room. 'Merry Christmas!'

'And to you, too.' Cece gave Millie a kiss on the cheek. 'Sorry I'm late for breakfast.'

'No need to be. I think there will be food flowing all day, thanks to Vivian. She's left so much for us.'

'I did say I would help serve though.'

'That's fine. Everyone helped themselves.'
Millie frowned at Cece's pale face and red eyes.
She looked like she'd been crying. 'Is everything
all right?'

'Yes, absolutely.'

'Are you sure? I'll listen if you have
something you wish to talk about. We can go
into my bedroom if you wish?'

'Oh no, no. I'm fine, truly.' Cece waved her
away and continued along the gallery, but Millie
wasn't convinced.

'Well, I'm here if you need me.'

Jeremy looked up at them from the bottom of
the stairs.

He was dressed in outdoor clothes. 'I was just
about to come up and look for you. It's time to
go to church. Adeline is grumbling about us
being late.'

Millie took a deep breath. 'Grandmama is
always grumbling about something lately. I
really don't know what's wrong with her. She's
never been one to be so... so crotchety.'

Jeremy grinned as they joined him. 'That's
one word for it.'

While Cece went to get her coat on, Millie
touched Jeremy's arm to prevent him from
walking away.

'What is it, my love?'

'I've told Nursé Allard to give Jonathan a
bottle later.' The guilt took hold of her once
again.

'Darling, he'll be fine. Look how well he has grown already?'

'Yes, I know…'

'And you're still going to feed him, aren't you?'

'Oh yes, this is just to add to that, to free up my time during the day. I'm so behind on everything.'

Jeremy kissed her. 'Jonathan will be fine.'

Millie nodded. One bottle a day wouldn't hurt Jonathan, and it would give her freedom to do all that she had to do.

Soon, the builders will return to finish rebuilding the chateau and then she'd have to organise the decorating of it, so that they could start entertaining the prominent people of the champagne world as was expected of them.

'You'd best get a hurry on, darling. Your grandmama is in a foul mood this morning.'

'Why? It's Christmas morning, for heaven's sake.'

Jeremy raised an eyebrow. 'I think she has got wind of your mama and Jacques enjoying each other's company and, as if that wasn't enough, apparently Stephen and Prue stayed up until very late drinking. They were found by your grandmama sleeping next to each other on the sofa in the Grand Salon this morning.' He shrugged as if to say it was all too much for him to handle.

'Good Lord, what is going on with my family right now?' Millie went down the corridor towards the room that held all their coats and boots, but as she passed the door to the kitchen she opened it and popped her head in. Daisy was standing at the table, bent over double.

'Daisy?' Millie went into the kitchen.

'Oh, madam.' Daisy's face screwed up in pain.

'Daisy! What is it?' Alarm made Millie's voice high.

'I think the baby is coming.' Daisy rubbed her large stomach.

The blood drained from Millie's face. Another early baby! 'Oh, good heavens. I'll get help. You're too early, as I was, but don't worry we have the incubator.'

'No, no, madam, I'm not.' Daisy puffed.

'I don't understand.' Millie was half ready to run for help.

'I'm due now.'

Millie tried to think straight. 'But you didn't get married until June... You're only six months, aren't you?'

Daisy groaned as another contraction hit her. 'No, madam, I'm due now. Royston and I... we didn't wait until we were married...'

'Oh, I see.' Millie was stumped for words.

'After Royston had been away with Sir Jeremy for so long in Plymouth, we missed each other so much and well, one thing led to another, you know how it is.'

Daisy wiped her hair away from her face. 'We thought it wouldn't matter as we were getting married, anyway. But I caught straight away. I was three months gone when I walked down the aisle.'

'Now it makes sense.' Millie gave Daisy a small smile as she looked at her round stomach. 'So, it's not an early baby then.'

'No, not in the slightest. Look at the size of me.' Daisy's face was a picture of surprise. 'I look like there's a dozen of them in there.'

Millie bit her lip to stop grinning. 'Yes, you're huge.'

'Madam!' Panic spread across Daisy's face. 'I'm getting another pain.'

'Go with it. You'll be fine,' Millie soothed and helped her to sit on a chair. 'I shall send for Royston.'

At that moment Jeremy came into the kitchen. 'My love, we are all waiting!'

'I'm sorry, but Daisy is in labour. I'm staying with her.'

'Ah, right. Yes, good.' Jeremy hesitated, half turning to leave. 'Shall I get Royston?'

'He'll be no use to me, Sir Jeremy, thank you,' Daisy muttered between gritted teeth.

'Can you drop everyone off at the church and then go to Épernay and find Doctor Duguay, please?' Millie asked, putting the kettle on to boil.

'Yes, of course. Though it is Christmas Day, I don't think he'll appreciate being disturbed. He might tell us to find a midwife.'

'I don't mind having a midwife,' Daisy panted. 'That's all I'd have back in England.'

Millie rubbed Daisy's back. 'I'm sure the doctor won't mind coming out. He was very good when Jonathan was born, but a midwife from the village is fine, too.'

'I'll be back as quick as I can.' Jeremy dashed from the room just as Royston came through the back door walking backwards carrying a crate of logs.

'Is the kettle on, lass?' he asked Daisy before realising that Millie was in the room. 'Oh, I say. What's going on here?'

'Your wife is in labour, Royston.' Millie smiled.

'Nay, lass. I've only been out of the room twenty minutes.'

'I've been uncomfortable all night.' Daisy closed her eyes as another pain hit.

Millie frowned, glancing at the clock on the wall. 'Your contractions are rather close, Daisy. How long have you been having them?'

'I don't know, madam. I've not felt great since yesterday.'

'Nay, lass.' Royston reared back. 'Why didn't you say anything?

'Because it wouldn't change anything would it?' she defended angrily. 'Women carrying babies have twinges and things all the time. It's normal. Me mam said so, and she'd know as she had ten of us.'

Royston stared at Millie. 'Shall I take her home, madam?'

'I think that is best, yes.' Millie eased Daisy to her feet. 'Can you make it to your cottage?'

'Yes, madam.' Daisy gripped the edge of the table as another pain bent her double.

'Another one?' Millie asked, feeling a little edgy.

Daisy sank to her knees with a low groan.

'She'll not make it to your cottage,' Millie said, knowing that to reach their cottage on the other side of the estate's orchard would mean Daisy would have to walk several hundred yards in the snow and cold.

'I can do it…' Daisy panted.

Millie paced, thinking. Every bedroom that was habitable was in use by her family. The rooms downstairs weren't suitable and in an hour the family would be back from church and wanting to open presents.

'I'll carry her, madam,' Royston said.

'Nonsense. We can't have you doing that, you might stumble and fall. She's heavy.'

Daisy grunted at the insult.

Millie pulled her thoughts into order. 'I know where we can take her. Vivian's room.'

'I couldn't, madam.'

'It's the perfect solution. Come along.' Millie and Royston half walked and half carried Daisy into the little room Vivian sometimes slept in when she stayed over sometimes instead of walking back to the village late at night. The room opposite the boot room was small but had a working fireplace and a small single bed.

Once they had Daisy sat on a wooden chair, Royston ran out to collect wood and paper to light a fire, while Millie stripped the bed and covered it with an old blanket she found in the cupboard.

Next, she went into the boot room and found an empty hessian sack and brought that in to place under the blanket to protect the mattress. She then helped Daisy onto the bed and covered her with a blanket.

'I'll make some tea. This might take a while,' Millie soothed before going back into the kitchen.

She quickly made the tea and took them into the room.

'Will the doctor come in time?' Daisy groaned and lifted her knees up. 'I feel something is happening.'

'What do you mean?' Panicked, Millie lifted Daisy's dress up and pulled down her underwear. She stared between Daisy's legs trying to work out what she was seeing.

'I need to push!' Daisy strained.

Millie's eyes widened as she saw the baby's head emerge with a crown of black hair. 'Daisy, the baby! It's coming!' She felt faint at the thought of it happening so soon.

Daisy moaned deep in her chest.

Heart racing, Millie didn't know what to do.

'I'll get a nice fire going,' Royston said, coming into the room. Only, on seeing between Daisy's legs, he dropped the armful of logs he held. 'Good God! The baby is coming!'

'What do we do?' Millie asked him.

Royston lost what colour he had in his face and gripped the door for support. 'I don't know! I've never delivered a baby before.'

Daisy started crying with worry. 'Help me.' She grabbed her legs and pushed again. 'Where's the midwife?'

Millie dithered, not knowing whether to run for help or do something with the baby.

Instinct took over, and she bent over the bed and held the baby's head as Daisy pushed again. 'Get me some towels, Royston, quickly!'

'Yes!' Royston dashed out of the door.

'That's good, Daisy. Everything is fine,' Millie soothed, though in truth she had no idea what to do. She didn't want to be responsible for this birth. What if something went wrong?

Royston hurtled back into the room and flung kitchen towels onto the bed. 'What else?'

'Build the fire, for God's sake!' Mille snapped, feeling the cold in the room.

Had she done wrong bringing them in here? Should they have just gone into the Grand Salon or dining room instead where fires were lit? What if the room was too cold for the baby? Despair filled her as Daisy pushed again. The baby inched its way out into the world. Millie held its little head, easing its shoulders out as Daisy groaned and gave little yelps.

'It's coming, Daisy,' Millie encouraged.

She concentrated on the baby and a steely resolve filled her that nothing would go wrong.

She was going to make sure both Daisy and the baby would make it through safely.

'It hurts,' Daisy ground out between clenched teeth as she pushed.

'I know it does, but it'll be all over soon.' Millie felt the baby's shoulders and held them, she gave a little pull and then in a swoosh of water and blood the baby slithered out onto the bed and its cry filled the room.

'It's here!' Royston, a piece of wood in his hand, stood staring in awe. He dropped the wood and fell to the floor beside the bed, kissing Daisy's face in rapture.

'What is it?' Daisy asked tiredly.

'A girl,' Millie said over the baby's wailing. She wiped the baby's tiny face, cleaning away the gunky birth mess. 'She's beautiful, Daisy.'

'She is all right?'

Millie checked her over as she carefully wrapped her up in another clean towel. 'Yes, she looks perfect to me and she's mighty loud.'

'Can I hold her?'

'Yes, but the cord is still attached...' Millie gently handed the precious bundle over to Daisy. 'We'll have to wait for the doctor. I can't do the afterbirth.' Millie's hands shook as she threw the blanket over both mother and baby as the new parents gazed adoringly at their baby.

Now the drama was over, Millie felt the need to sit down, her legs were a little wobbly.

'You've done so well, Lady Remington,' Royston said, beaming. 'Thank you very much!'

'Daisy did all the hard work.' Millie slipped off the bed. 'I'm going to make fresh cups of tea for us all. That fire needs attending to, though. It's cold in here.'

'I'll have it started in a jiffy.' Royston jumped to the task.

'Don't move, Daisy. The doctor or a midwife should be here soon.'

As Royston saw to the fire, Millie left them and went into the kitchen. She added more wood to the range and filled the large kettle with water from the tap in the scullery. In the distance she heard the church bells ringing.

She was halfway through setting up a tray when she sat down on a chair and burst into tears.

'Millie!' Jeremy hurried into the kitchen, his expression anxious. 'Darling?' He held her to him.

'I'm all right, really.'

'What's happened?'

'It's a baby girl.' Millie looked at him through tear-filled eyes. 'I've just brought a baby into the world. I was so scared, Jeremy.'

'Naturally you would be, my love, but you did it. Mother and baby are all good now, aren't they?'

She nodded and finding a handkerchief from her pocket she blew her nose. 'Yes, they seem to be.'

'Well then.' He kissed her, smiling tenderly. 'You've done a wonderful thing. I'm so proud of you.' He gave her another kiss. 'Shall I make the tea? The midwife is coming from the village. I met her at the church when I dropped everyone off and she said she'd go home and get her bag of tricks and her husband will bring her here. Though it's a wasted journey now, isn't it?'

'No, there's the afterbirth to deliver.'

Jeremy mashed the tea leaves. 'Well, I'll stay down here and sort them all out. Why don't you go upstairs and have a lie down for a little bit and I'll bring you up some tea.'

'Thank you, that would be wonderful.' She still felt shaky.

'The family will be back soon, and it'll be a busy afternoon with opening presents and Prue wants us to play charades and have dancing.' Jeremy shook his head. 'That sister of yours is exhausting. Where does she get her energy from?'

'No idea.' Millie smiled at the thought of Prue's enthusiasm, but then her mind turned to Cece and the sadness that covered her like a cloak. Something was troubling her, and she needed to find out what.

Chapter Seven

Prue sat forward on the sofa eagerly watching Stephen mime the book title he was describing in the charades game they were playing. It was on the tip of her tongue what the book was, but Stephen was so funny with his acting that she kept giggling at his antics and not concentrating.

'*Wuthering Heights,*' Mama announced.

'How could it possibly be that?' Grandmama frowned at her daughter. 'Have sense.'

Mama shrugged and held her glass out to be filled with the wine Jacques was distributing. 'I thought it might be, that's all.'

Prue laughed. 'Good try, Mama.' She turned to Cece. 'What do you think it is?'

Cece glanced up from a magazine she was flipping through. 'I don't know nor care.'

'What's wrong with you?' Prue demanded. All day Cece had been sullen and irritating. 'You've a face like you've sucked a lemon.'

'*A Christmas Carol!*' Monty suddenly shouted, diverting her attention from Cece and back to the game.

'Yes, that's correct!' Stephen laughed. 'Finally.' He looked at Prue. 'You should have got that one.'

'I was trying!' She grinned. 'You've not a very good actor.'

'I did my best. We're losing now.' He slumped on the sofa beside her.

Vivian and the girls, having returned from their homes, came in carrying trays of coffee, tea and delicious pastries. It was late evening on Christmas Day and a good mood filled the chateau, if they ignored Cece's grumpiness. Presents had been opened earlier after everyone had gone in to see the newest addition to the estate. Despite only being a lady's maid back in England, Daisy had been a valued member of the Marsh staff for years and Prue and Cece were eager to see the little baby before Daisy and Royston left for their cottage.

As coffee and tea were poured and circulated, Prue grabbed a plate of pastries and passed it to Stephen.

'Are you trying to make me fat, Miss Marsh?' he joked.

She grinned, liking the flirting they'd been doing for the last couple of days. Stephen was dashing and cheeky, an officer who'd been through a war and who had come out of it whole and with a sense of feeling that life was too short to be serious. She liked that about him. Her family could be so stuffy sometimes and she enjoyed his sense of fun.

Last night they had stayed up late when everyone went to bed.

Just the two of them they had drank bottles of champagne and told each other stories, they'd shared secrets and dreams and a few stolen kisses before she'd fallen asleep on his shoulder. It had been a delightful night. Although the looks of disapproval from her mama and grandmama this morning hadn't helped her deal with a banging headache.

'What about some dancing?' Monty suggested.

'Yes!' Prue put her coffee down and jumped up. 'I bought Millie those new records for her present, I'm sure she won't mind us playing them now.'

'But she's not down here to listen to them.' Monty went with her to the gramophone in the corner.

'Millie won't mind, she and Jeremy are busy settling Daisy and the baby in the cottage. By the time they come back, they'll likely go straight up to spend time with Jonathan and then to bed.' Prue sorted through the records.

'It's common decency to ask first, Prue,' Cece snapped. 'They aren't yours.'

Taking a deep breath, Prue faced her sister. 'As if Millie would mind, honestly.'

'Oh, do what you want, you always do!' Cece stormed from the room.

Mama glared at Prue. 'What have you done to upset her now?'

'Nothing!' Prue defended. 'I'm so tired of her moods! I'm having it out with her.' She marched from the room even though Mama called her back.

Cece's sniping and cold rebuffs were wearing on her patience. Upstairs, she stomped along the gallery to their shared bedroom and flung open the door.

Sitting on the bed, Cece's head snapped up. 'Go away.'

'I will not!' Prue stood at the end of the bed, her fists clenched. 'I demand you tell me what is wrong. I have done nothing to you and yet you've treated me all holidays as though I'm someone beneath you. I'm tired of your catty remarks and your snide comments. So out with it!'

'Stop yelling, you'll wake Jonathan up.'

'I don't care. I'm not spending another moment in your company without you telling me what the hell is going on with you.'

'It's *nothing.*'

'It's *something* because you're not being you. You don't smile or laugh any more. What have I done that is so bad that you are like this?'

'It's not something you've done. Not everything is about *you*, Prue!'

That admission took the heat from her argument. Prue frowned, her mind trying to work out the problem. 'If it's not me, then who?'

'It doesn't matter.'

'It does.' Prue sat on the bed beside Cece. 'Out with it. Now. I'm done with guessing games, it's childish. Talk to me as an adult.'

'There's nothing to talk about. Not really.'

'Cece!' Prue wanted to throttle her.

Sighing, Cece walked to the window and stared out at the black night. 'You already know half of it anyway, or half guessed.'

'Which is?'

'I am in love with Monty.'

'Yes, I do know that.'

Cece spun around. 'And I suppose you have an opinion on that as well?'

'Of course,' Prue said flippantly. 'You hardly hid the fact, did you? So, it's going to cause comment.'

'Who else knows?'

'Millie, naturally.'

'Dear Lord.'

'He's not going to help you.' Prue folded her arms. 'Millie and I could see how you felt about Monty at Remington Court. The minute you met Monty you went all doe-eyed and soft about him. Then when you mentioned you were both going to exchange letters once we went back to York, well it was obvious you'd fallen for him.'

'How you and Millie must have laughed at me.'

'Laughed?' Prue tilted her head and stared at her.

'Why on earth would we laugh at you? He is the man you want, and who are we to say otherwise? Millie did have some concerns at the beginning as we knew nothing about Monty, but Jeremy liked and trusted him, and then later, Monty told Millie about his background. He's a good man. I like him.'

'You would!'

'What does that mean?'

'You're too free with your flirting. Anyone wearing trousers gets your attention.'

'And? Flirting isn't harmful, Cece. You should lighten up and try it sometime. It's rather fun.'

'It wouldn't work for me now, anyway.'

'I don't understand.'

Cece sighed and closed her eyes momentarily. 'Monty doesn't return my feelings.'

'How do you know?'

'I asked him.'

'Oh, dear.'

'I thought he might have fallen in love with you.'

'Me?' This shocked Prue. 'I don't want Monty, I promise you. I simply flirt, that's all. Nothing is meant by it, you know that.'

'That's just as well as he doesn't want you either. I got that wrong, too.'

'Gosh, that's a relief.' Prue let out a breath. The last thing she wanted was unrequited attention from Monty.

'He is in love with Millie.'

'No!'

'Yes. Though he says he's unsure about what he feels exactly.'

Shocked, Prue leapt to her feet. 'Millie loves Jeremy. She'd not look at Monty in any way other than a friend. Jeremy and Jonathan are her life.'

'He knows that.' Cece looked down at her hands. 'I feel a little sorry for him in a way, for I know how it feels to want someone you can't have.'

'Cece, I'm so sorry.' Prue went and put her arms around her sister.

'I'm finding it difficult to be around him now.'

'True, it would be difficult. *Horribly* difficult.'

'I feel so ridiculous.'

'It's not your fault. You just need to forget about him.'

'Easier said than done.'

'But soon we will be returning to York, and he will go to Remington Court. You'll not have to see him.'

Cece slumped onto the bed. 'Do you ever feel that life is passing you by?'

Prue hid a yawn behind her hand. 'Not really. Well… maybe. A little.' She crossed to her own bed and lay down on it and stared up at the ceiling. 'That's a lie. I feel it all the time. I'm aching for something to happen in my life.'

'Me, too.' Cece kicked off her shoes. 'Sometimes I feel like nothing will ever happen to me. That I'll grow old just accompanying Mama around York doing good work with charities, going to music recitals, the odd dinner party, you know?'

'I do know, and that's not happening to me!' Prue studied her. 'I never thought you were one to hanker after excitement.'

'I don't want drama, not like you. But everyone assumes I'm happy to be dull.'

'And are you? Because if you're not only you can change that. I don't want drama, either, not in a bad way. I just want excitement, to feel alive. Surely, that's not so horrendous?'

'No.'

'It's perfectly acceptable to want different things, Cece,' Prue murmured. 'We are different people. We just have to find our own way, follow our own paths.'

Cece looked at her. 'Aren't you scared you'll get it wrong?'

Prue grinned. 'That's probably part of the fun!'

Chapter Eight

Millie sat in the rocking chair by the window in the nursery with Jonathan asleep in her arms. It was the day after Boxing Day and the house was a little quieter. This morning had seen the departures of Stephen, who had returned to his unit, and Monty, who had gone back to Remington Court in Yorkshire.

She glanced up as Mama walked in.

'I'm sorry, my dear, I don't want to disturb you.'

'You aren't. This little man is fast asleep, and I didn't want to part with him just yet.'

Mama looked around. 'Where's the nanny?'

'Down in the kitchen having her meal.' Millie watched Mama stroll around the room, touching the odd thing, folding a blanket. She seemed ill at ease. 'Mama is something troubling you?'

'No, no, not really.'

Millie waited, allowing the silence to linger. When a log shifted in the grate, sending sparks up the chimney, Mama went to the window and looked out.

'This is a beautiful home, Millie. You've done so well to rebuild and redecorate as you have in such a short time.'

'There's still much to be done, as you can see. The whole right wing of the chateau needs repairing, and the business needs expanding to become profitable.'

Mama snorted. 'I think we have drunk the profits in the time we've been here.'

Millie smiled and moved Jonathan in her arms a little. 'It's a good thing the estate manager hid bottles during the war.'

'That's Pascal, isn't it, the little unkempt man who runs about the estate doing numerous jobs at once.'

Laughing gently, Millie stood. 'That's him, yes.'

'Jacques praises him constantly. What that man doesn't know about champagne isn't worth knowing, apparently.'

Millie paused in placing Jonathan in the incubator but didn't say anything. Lately, Mama couldn't have a conversation without mentioning Jacques.

'You don't approve, do you?' Mama asked.

'Approve of what?'

'Don't play silly with me. Jacques told me he has spoken to you about him and me.'

Fussing with settling Jonathan, Millie kept her gaze averted.

'Millie, I wish to talk to you about the situation, as I can't talk to my own mother, who is acting as though I'm running away to join a circus.'

'What is it that you are actually doing, Mama?' Millie closed the glass front of the incubator.

'He is my friend.'

Millie folded her arms, prepared to listen. 'You're allowed to have friends.'

'Jacques is not free…'

'No.'

'And nor am I, not really.' Mama fiddled with a little knitted jacket that was sitting on top of a set of drawers.

'What do you mean?'

'Your papa isn't long gone.'

'No.'

'It is too soon for me to think of anyone else.'

'Is Jacques pressuring you?' Millie was instantly defensive.

Mama spun around. 'No! No, not at all. He's not like that, you know he isn't.'

'Then what are you saying?'

'I don't know. I suppose I wanted your blessing should I decide to continue our friendship…'

'Which may lead to something more, is that it?'

'Perhaps, in time. Jacques has much to deal with himself. His wife, getting a divorce, which will paint him as a bad person to society. I've told him a divorce is the only option if he wants me in his life. I will not be seen as the scarlet woman!'

'I think the French, especially Parisians, are rather broad-minded when it comes to love and affairs.'

'I'll not be having an affair, Millie!' Mama looked outraged at the thought.

'If you're not, then I don't understand why you are worried? Be friends for a couple of years until Jacques sorts out his situation with his wife. By the sounds of it she wants to be free as much as he does.'

'Yes, it seems so. But then there is this situation with Jeremy. Jacques so wants a relationship with his son, Millie. I can't tell you how much it pains him that Jeremy is distant with him.'

'Jeremy is doing the best he can. We've had an enormous adjustment coming to the chateau, rebuilding, Jonathan's early birth and finding out Jeremy's true parentage. It's been difficult for all concerned.'

'Yes, I know.' Mama sighed. 'Life is not so easy at times.'

Millie watched the emotions play on her mother's face. 'You have my blessing, Mama. I don't want you to spend the rest of your life alone. None of us want that.'

'I think my mother does.'

'Grandmama is being selfish,' Millie scoffed.

'Since Grandpapa died she has lived either in London surrounded by her friends and having the time of her life, or she's in York with you and having all of us running around after her and keeping her entertained. She doesn't want that to change.'

'Jacques mentioned that I'd have to come to live in Paris, as he can't leave. He wants to build the business with Jeremy and he won't let him down. He feels he has so much to make up for.'

'And do you feel you couldn't live in Paris?'

'But what of Prue and Cece?'

'What of them? They are grown women, Mama, not children. Let them decide what they want. You have to be happy and if being with Jacques, in time, makes you happy then do it.'

Abruptly Prue was standing at the door. 'We only have one life to live, Mama.'

Cece stood next to her. 'We want you to be happy, Mama.'

Determination glowed in Mama's eyes. 'I'm not making any definite plans, not yet. It will take some time for me to think it through, and I'm still not used to not having your papa with me... But Jacques is a good man, and he makes me smile.'

'And laugh,' Prue added. 'We've not heard you laugh like you have done this Christmas in a very long time.'

Mama sighed. 'And I felt guilty doing so. Being with Jacques has made me feel as though I was being unfaithful to Lionel.'

'We all have to try and grab happiness when we can,' Cece said. 'Papa would want you to be happy.'

Millie embraced Mama, and Prue and Cece joined in. 'Now all we have to do is convince Grandmama!'

~ ~ ~ ~

From the front door steps, Millie supervised the loading of the luggage onto the truck, which Pascal would drive to Calais while Grandmama, Prue and Cece were to go with Royston in Jeremy's motor car. Following them, Jacques would be in his little sports car with Mama. It was decided that Jeremy wouldn't drive them to the port, so Millie wouldn't be alone, and she was glad they'd made that decision. The chateau would be quiet without them all.

The wind had died down, and the snow had melted into piles of slush. Although cold, the sky was blue and clear. Pascal and Royston were stacking and tying down suitcases, while inside the family were saying final goodbyes and donning coats and hats.

'When will you be coming back to England?' Grandmama inquired, coming to stand beside Millie.

'Not for some time. We have so much to do here, and Jonathan is too little.'

Grandmama nodded and pulled on her fur-lined gloves. 'To think I have a little French great-grandson, it's still hard to imagine. But don't make him *too* French, will you? He needs to know he's English as well.'

'Jonathan will have the best of both worlds.'

'I've put him in my will.'

'Thank you, Grandmama.'

'There are stipulations, of course.' Grandmama's expression became fierce. 'I'll not have him using the money to buy German made goods, property in Germany, or buy German businesses.'

'Golly, that's rather an extreme ruling, why not?'

'Because the Germans aren't finished with us yet, my dear. You can count on that.'

'Germany is broken. We won two years ago.'

'Don't be naive, girl,' Grandmama scoffed. 'Keep your eyes and ears open. Read the papers. You're close to the German border, you need to keep your wits about you.'

'Nothing will happen again with Germany, they are done for.'

'All I'm saying is keep an open mind. I have a great many friends in high places and I feel Germany is only licking its wounds. One day they might rise again.'

'Well, I hope that's not for a very long time, if ever.' Millie shuddered at the thought.

Grandmama gave a long sigh. 'Forgive me, Millie. I fear I have been a trifle quarrelsome these last few weeks, my dear, and I apologise.'

Millie stared at her. Grandmama never apologised for anything.

'I am old, my girl. The older I get, the more set in my ways I'm becoming, and I hate that.' Grandmama gazed into the distance. 'I've been an adventurer all my life, a rule breaker at times. However, lately, I've had to face that time is moving on, I'm no longer the young woman I once was. Over Christmas I have been watching you all, and I have realised you are all grown women, each with your own lives to lead, including Violet.'

'Mama needs—'

'Let me finish.' Grandmama held up her hand. 'Let me finish before the others come out. I just want you to know, and I'll tell your sisters and mama, too, that I am enormously proud of all of you. I'm also a little envious.'

'Envious?'

'Yes, because you all have years ahead of you and I do not.'

'Grandmama…'

'Don't waste it, Millie. Don't waste the years. Make them count. Promise me.'

'I promise.'

'Good.' Satisfied, Grandmama took a deep breath. 'I'm looking forward to going home, but I feel your sisters are at a loose end, as the saying goes.'

Millie gave a sad smile, knowing she'd miss them all so much. 'They will need your guidance, as will Mama.'

'Huh!' Grandmama huffed. 'As if they'd listen to me.' She looked out the corner of her eye at Millie. 'But you're right. They need me, and I'm not dead yet. There is still a little more I wish to do in my life.'

As the others came out, a sombreness pervaded each and everyone one of them and tears gathered.

Grandmama tutted at them. 'Stop your crying. Anyone would think we are going to a funeral.' She climbed into the motor car. 'We'll be back soon enough, Millie dear.'

Hugs and kisses were exchanged and reminders to write often.

Prue held Millie tightly. 'I'll write.'

'Yes, do, I want to know everything you get up to!'

Smiling brightly, Prue lifted her head regally. 'I can't tell you *everything* for I plan on being a little bit naughty!'

Shaking her head with a smile, Millie turned to Cece. 'If you need me I'm here. Come back whenever you wish.'

'Thank you.'

'Find some happiness,' Millie whispered as she hugged Cece.

'I'll try.'

Millie stood away from the motor car, wiping away tears as Prue and Cece waved from inside the car.

Jacques came beside her and kissed her cheeks. 'I'll be back in a few weeks, *mon cher.*'

'Wonderful. I'll look forward to it. Drive carefully.'

He shook Jeremy's hand. 'You'll come to Paris next week for a meeting?'

'I will,' Jeremy answered. 'We have much to sort out with finding new markets.'

Mama embraced Jeremy and then Millie. 'Write to me every week. I think I'll come back in the summer though, if you don't mind? I don't want Jonathan growing up without knowing who I am.'

Millie smiled. 'Yes, that is a wonderful idea. Come whenever you like.'

When at last the vehicles drove down the driveway, Jeremy hugged Millie close to his side. 'Just the three of us again.'

'And a dozen estate workers, and inside staff, but yes, it's just the three of us again,' she joked.

'I know you'll miss your family.'

'Yes, I will, but the two main people in my life are right here. And I expect I'm going to be very busy.'

'No regrets for marrying a damaged ex-army officer and coming to his equally damaged chateau?' Jeremy asked quietly.

'None at all.' She reached up and kissed him.

Arm in arm, they walked back up the steps. 'I think we should get a dog, or maybe two,' he said suddenly.

'Oh, Jeremy!'

Author Note

Hello Readers,

I hope you enjoyed this novella which is an accompaniment of Millie - book one of this new Marsh Saga series.

If you haven't yet read Millie, I've put a taster below.

Millie was a new era for me to write. I'd never written a story set in the 1920s before and had to research a lot about how women were stretching the boundaries of their independence and freedom. The end of WWI brought many changes, but at the bottom of it all, women were still expected to marry well and raise children. I wanted that for Millie because she is the oldest and would naturally lead the way for her sisters. Yet, I also wanted to show each sister as being unique.

Millie was a joy to write and I hope you liked meeting the Marsh family. I've added a short excerpt of the next book, which is about Prue, Millie's sister you met in book one and in this novella. After *Prue*, there will be Cece's story, and also Alice's story, Prue's friend – you will meet her soon.

Lastly, I plan to write another story which will be Grandmama's life, and how she defied the Victorian rules to be her own woman. She is such a great character I couldn't leave her out!

AnneMarie Brear
2019.

Millie

Chapter One

Yorkshire, England
Late August 1919

Millie lightly touched the white rosebuds in her short black curly hair. She smiled at her maid's reflection in the oval mirror. 'You've done a wonderful job of it, Daisy. Thank you.'

'I'm so pleased you like it, miss. It has to be perfect for today of all days.' Daisy, small and thin, fussed with Millie's hair a bit more, tweaking a rosebud or two.

'Are you all packed?' She watched Daisy thread another pearl stud hairpin into place.

'Yes, miss. It's all downstairs ready to go to the station.'

'And you said farewell to your family?'

'I have, miss.' Daisy's smile didn't waver. 'My mother will be at the church, anyway, miss, to see you on this important day.'

'That's so kind of her.'

'The whole village is coming out I should think. It's not often one of the important families of the area gets married in the local church. They want to send you off with their best wishes. You're the first Marsh girl to be married.'

'I'll be happy to see them, and I couldn't have married anywhere else. Prue suggested York Minster, but that's too formal. I wanted to marry in the village, as it's home.' Excitement bubbled up in her chest. She was getting married! She hardly believed it.

'I'm pleased you're having the wedding breakfast here at Elm House, and not in a reception room in York.' Daisy sighed happily. 'It's all so beautiful.'

'And the sun is shining!' Millie laughed, opening a small brown velvet box. Inside, diamond earrings glittered, a gift from her intended groom. It was so thoughtful of him and unexpected. She paused a moment and thought of Jeremy, the man she was to marry in under an hour.

How had it happened so fast? A man she'd known for years, but never really thought of as husband material, had never really thought of him as someone other than her father's friend. A man she had seen at every social event, and at most times seated along the family dining table here at home.

Lifting the earrings from their satin bed, she admired them in the morning light.

'They are lovely, miss.' Daisy sighed dreamily, staring at them.

'I am most fortunate.' Donning them, Millie's gaze went to the door as it opened and in came her two sisters, Prudence and Cecilia, and their cousin, Agatha. Excited voices filled the room as they circled around Millie where she sat at her dressing table.

'You look like an angel, Millie,' Agatha said softly, hesitant as always to make herself known. Their mousy cousin happily followed in the Marsh girls' wake.

'I doubt that but thank you.' She gazed at their dresses of palest blue satin. 'You all look lovely, too.'

'This is the saddest day of my life!' Prue, always dramatic, flopped onto the bed and hugged a corner post forlornly. 'I cannot believe that tonight this room will be empty forever. You'll never be just down the hallway, or at your place at the breakfast table. Why must you marry? Is it because of the shortage of men after the war? You'll not be left on the shelf you know, not you. You're too pretty, too *good,* to be overlooked by the men who did come back.'

She tossed her pretty head angrily. 'That bloody war. And I will say *bloody* because that's what it was. Destroying families, our whole generation of fine young men, or maiming them beyond any use to anyone!'

'Prue!' Cece gaped, her face paling, if that was possible with her porcelain skin which held a hint of freckles that she hated almost as much as her red hair, a legacy from their father. 'Do be quiet. That is cruel. It's not their fault. When I think of those poor men, our *friends*, who will never be the same. It fair breaks my heart.'

Prue sat up indignantly. 'You know I saw Robbie Simmons the other day in the village? Blind. I couldn't, *wouldn't* believe it. He was jolly enough, of course, but I was beside myself with the pain of it. And he could ride so well, and shoot, and now what has he got?'

'Some lovely girl will fall in love with him,' Agatha said softly. 'Some people can see past things like that.'

'Yes, some can, I suppose, but what if the rest of us can't?' Prue snapped. 'Then suddenly it is *we* who are awful with no compassion. It's a disgrace.' She turned back to Millie. 'So, is that why you said yes to Sir Jeremy? Because he came back whole? Well, nearly whole. They say he's even quieter than ever, *tormented*, perhaps, by what he's seen and done.'

'Prue, please,' Cece murmured, giving Millie a horrified look.

'That's enough, Prue. We've been through this.' Millie glared at her sister. 'Do you wish to ruin my day?'

'No... But really, Millie. Why not marry someone young and dashing? There are some left, I assure you. Pick one of our friends instead of Sir Jeremy Remington. Tom Rollings and Henry Pinkerton both came back without a scratch and so did Arthur Healy and —'

'Prue!' Cece's warning went unheeded as Prue launched into another rant on why marrying Sir Jeremy was the wrong thing to do.

'But he's *so* old.' Prue protested, tossing her head, obviously not caring if her hairpins fell out.

'He's thirty-six.' Millie spread her hands out in protest. Anyone over the age of twenty-one was old to Prue.

'He lives in a crumbling old manor in the middle of nowhere.'

'No, he doesn't. Remington Court is perfectly fine. It's the chateau in Northern France that isn't so good. Since his Uncle Louis's death and the German occupation of it, it is in a bad state.'

'And we'll never see you!'

'I'll be only twenty miles away. We will see each other all the time.'

'He's father's friend, not ours.'

'We've all known him for years. And you,' she pointed a finger at Prue, 'have always got on well with him!'

'Yes, I do, but it doesn't mean I'd marry him!' Her blue eyes so like Millie's flashed defiantly.

'He didn't ask you.'

'Well, you cannot deny that he's sour. I swear I've never seen him laugh. All we get are twitches of his lips when something is amusing. He's handsome enough I suppose, if you like them to be cold and distant with it.'

Agatha twitched her skirt. 'Millie has her very own Mr Darcy.'

'Don't talk nonsense, Agatha. Mr Darcy indeed. Everything is not like you read in those infernal books of yours.' Prue glared. 'Millie can do so much better!'

'Prudence Violet Mary Marsh.' Their mother's voice from the doorway had them all turning to her.

Prue flushed guiltily.

Millie is available in Kindle and paperback.

Prue

Chapter One

London, 1921.

Prue Marsh sauntered through the elegant shop belonging to Mrs Eve Yolland, dressmaker. The walls of dark mahogany shelving held bolts of material; linen, cotton, silk, damask, crepe georgette, velveteen and wool. The colours were arranged in shades from light to dark from white to black and every shade in between. Excellent light came from the large front windows facing the street, illuminating the tasteful, and discreet arrangement of accessories any woman should have the need to purchase. Assortments of beaded bags, satin purses, lawn handkerchiefs, kidskin gloves, jewelled headdresses, fans and shimmering shawls drew Prue's attention. But today, her hands merely drifted over the displayed finery, her mind wondering.

Restless.

She was always restless. Her mama said she needed a husband and a house to organise, but such mundane options failed to inspire her. And that was the problem. She wasn't inspired by anything at the moment. Summer was fast approaching, and invitations were arriving at Elm Court, her home in York, thick and fast for all sorts of entertainment like garden parties, social dances, private dinners, musical soirees, house parties and picnics, but she'd meet the same people again, the people she'd known all he life and it wasn't enough.

So, she'd left Mama and her younger sister Cece and escaped to London to stay with her grandmama and hope the London scene would be more entertaining.

'Prue!' Grandmama's raised eyebrows and sharp look snapped her back to the present.

'Sorry. What did you say?'

Her grandmama, Adeline Fordham, was not one to ignore, even if it was unintentional. Grandmama led the way to the shop's entrance. 'I asked if you needed more time or are you happy to move on?'

'I'm finished.' She nodded her goodbyes to Eve Yolland and her assistants, before leaving the building and stepping into the brand-new motor car waiting at the curb side. The dark green Sunbeam, Grandmama's latest acquisition, shone like a new penny in the sunshine.

Once Higgins, the chauffeur, closed the door and climbed behind the wheel, Prue settled back against the leather seat.

'Right. Enough.' Grandmama peered at her. 'I refuse to spend another moment with you in this mood. What is the matter? For weeks you've been walking around London as though some great misfortune has befallen you. I insist on knowing the cause of it, or you can go back to your mama in Yorkshire.'

'I'm fine. Tell Higgins where we need to go, Grandmama.'

'Home, Higgins, if you please.'

'Home?' Prue frowned. 'I thought we had another appointment?'

'We do or did. But this is more important. So, you can either talk on the way home, or if it is of a delicate nature,' she directed at look at the back of Higgin's head, 'we shall wait until we are behind closed doors.'

'There is nothing to talk about.' Prue stared at the passing people walking along the streets of Westminster.

'I beg to differ.' The superior expression on Grandmama's face was familiar. 'You are depressing me, girl, and if I wanted to be depressed, I'd visit my neighbour, Felix Truman, and listen to him talk about his collection of snails! Why a man in his eighties wishes to have a collection of snails is beyond me. You can't pass him in the street without receiving a lecture on his latest procurements. So, out with it.'

Sighing heavily, Prue knew she'd not easily divert her when she had the bit between her teeth. 'Honestly, Grandmama, nothing has happened.' She shrugged one shoulder, a feeling of hopelessness descending again. It shocked her more than anyone that she felt like this. Never in her life had she been so uninterested in anything. Frankly, it worried her. She was always the one in the family to start a party, or a game. She felt that laughing and having fun was the only way to be. She left being serious to Cece, who'd made it into an art form and bored everyone with her stuffiness, and Millie, her older sister had the homely attributes for being a wife and mother that suited her perfectly. Yet, Prue knew she wasn't ready for any of that.

'Ah, of course.' Grandmama patted Prue's knee, nodding her head wisely. 'I understand now. Silly of me not to see it before.'

'See what?' She turned to look out the window at the passing rows of houses as they entered Mayfair, where the Grandmama's townhouse was situated.

It took a moment for Grandmama to turn back to her, and when she did a small smile played about her lips. 'I forgot how much like me you are. Millie has my strength, but in a quiet, efficient way, and Cece has my kindness and sweet nature, but you, you have my restive character, my spirit of adventure. I should have done something about it earlier.'

Prue grinned at Grandmama declaring her sweet nature. There was nothing sweet about Grandmama. Adeline Fordham was known for speaking her mind and didn't suffer fools gladly. Prue glanced out the window as clouds skidded over the sun. 'Done something about it what? Whatever do you mean?'

'The war interrupted things, but everything is settling down once again now. It's time.'

Higgins slowed the automobile in front of the white-painted terraced house and Kilburn, the butler, rushed out to open the motor car door.

Alighting, Prue waited for Grandmama to accompany her up the three short steps to the shiny black front door. 'You're talking in riddles. Time for what?'

'Why, to take you abroad, properly, not just to Millie's chateau in France.'

'Abroad?' Following her into the parlour, Prue slipped off her gloves, wondering if she'd heard correctly. No one went abroad now, or hadn't done for years, not since the war started in '14 and then afterwards the Spanish Flu epidemic had decimated hundreds of thousands of people and Europe had plunged into greyness. There was no incentive to travel to countries fighting bankruptcy and restrictions.

'It's high time we sampled the delectable delights of travelling to other places, my dear.

High time indeed. And *you* especially.' She sat down at her rosewood desk in the corner and selected several sheets of writing paper. 'You, my dear, need to explore the world as I did before I married. There's nothing better than experiencing foreign cities and people. It broadens one's mind.'

A bud of excitement grew in the pit of Prue's stomach. Abroad. Travelling. Yes. Absolutely, yes. 'When can we go, Grandmama?'

Prue will be available in 2020 in Kindle and paperback.

Acknowledgements

Thank you to my editor, Jane Eastgate, thank you for finding my mistakes when I think there are none!

To my talented cover designer, Evelyn Labelle, you always give me what I want, thank you!

Thank you to my family and friends. Your support means the world to me, especially my husband.

Finally, the biggest thank you goes to my readers. Over the years I have received the most wonderful messages from readers who have told me how much they've enjoyed my stories. Each and every message and review encourages me to write the next book.

Most authors go through times when they think the story they are writing is no good and I am no exception. The times when we struggle with the plot, when the characters don't behave as we wish them to, when 'normal' life interferes with the writing process and we feel we haven't got enough time in the day to do all we have to do those messages make us smile!

A few words from a stranger saying they loved my story dispels my doubts over my ability to be an author. I can't express enough how much those lovely messages mean to me. So, thank you!

If you'd like to receive my email newsletter, or find out more about me and my books, please go to my website where you can join the mailing list. http://www.annemariebrear.com

Say hello on my Facebook author page: http://www.facebook.com/annemariebrear